Vulture Wings

Infamous low-lives, the Strong brothers will do anything for a quick buck, but this was going to be no ordinary kidnap. They are paid to abduct two young men, and don't ask too many questions when their paymaster gives them some unusual instructions. Then as the boys' father races to rescue his sons, he realizes that their snatching is linked to dark secrets from his old life as a bounty hunter.

Vulture Wings

Dirk Hawkman

A Black Horse Western

ROBERT HALE

© Dirk Hawkman 2018
First published in Great Britain 2018

ISBN 978-0-7198-2751-8

The Crowood Press
The Stable Block
Crowood Lane
Ramsbury
Marlborough
Wiltshire SN8 2HR

www.bhwesterns.com

Robert Hale is an imprint
of The Crowood Press

Typeset by
Derek Doyle & Associates, Shaw Heath
Printed and bound in Great Britain by
4edge Limited

PROLOGUE

Enrique was a professional killer – not a babysitter. It seemed like an earlier incarnation when Enrique was a lowly rifleman in the Mexican army. Though he had learned how to handle a weapon, he had not learned how to obey the rules. Enrique had loathed the army's petty discipline, and deserted. Wyoming territory was as far away as he could get. There, Enrique found that there was much demand for his heartless ability to get a dirty job done.

He had arranged the disappearances of countless witnesses, and their later reappearances with torn throats. Enrique had a reputation for ruthless results. Perhaps he was too good at his job, for his boss had noted the assassin's ability as a fixer. Enrique never shied from dirty or difficult challenges. He was being asked to carry out more and more for his patron.

That was why he was riding into Crow Valley. Enrique never shirked, nor moaned. His boss paid him extremely well for his toxic talents. Inwardly, though, Enrique resented this particular errand. He had been instructed to get the Strong brothers out of jail. Again.

He had waited until nightfall. While he did not plan on any shooting, Enrique would pull the trigger if necessary. Murder, to Enrique, was like a painful extraction to a dentist. It was bloody and nasty for the casualty, but afterwards he would wash his hands and start the next job on his list. In any case, the sheriff of Crow Valley was a stooge of Enrique's. All Enrique had to do was hand over the bribe.

Crow Valley was sleepy that evening. It was almost midnight, and even the saloon was shut. Enrique spotted a few lights on, but otherwise the dull farming settlement was dormant. The Wyoming summer could be punishing, but the evenings were chilly. Enrique pulled his jacket tight to his skinny frame, but it did little to fight the cold air's touch. Except for the odd draught of wind, the town was silent.

He was not rushing. Enrique dismounted, and noticed a mirror attached to the wooden wall outside a store. He could not resist. Gloomy though it was, the moonlight was illumination enough for him to inspect his reflection. Enrique was not a vain man. Empty arrogance caused fatal slips of judgment. Rather, he was meticulous and highly disciplined. He took fastidious pride in his immaculate appearance. Though his reflection was shadowy in the gloom, Enrique grinned as he gave his neat moustache a little tweak.

It was time to press on with his tiresome chore, though. He crossed the dirt road to the sheriff's office. Politely, Enrique knocked on the door. The lawman inside well knew that he was in Enrique's thrall, but the killer rapped the door anyway. It would do no harm to keep up appearances.

The sheriff answered. He had been informed that Enrique would be calling on him, and had waited up accordingly. The lawman was hardly a dedicated enforcer of justice. Sheriff Green was perhaps forty years old, but looked much older. His hair was whitening prematurely, and his leather waistcoat strained to cover his prominent gut. Green was a weary man. Heavy drinking and too many late nights at the poker table were exhausting him. There were whispers in Crow Valley that the councilmen were going to dismiss their lazy lawman. Green's fears about his future employment, and his gambling debts, meant that he needed Enrique's money.

'Enrique,' Green greeted his visitor with a sigh. 'Come in.'

Enrique entered the bureau, and got straight down to business.

'Take me to the Strong brothers.'

'Money first.' Enrique fished the wedge of dollars from inside his jacket, and handed the cash over. Green glowered at Enrique with contempt, but took the money nonetheless. He counted the cash frantically. Enrique had spies in Crow Valley, and knew that within days, the sheriff would have squandered every last dollar.

'OK. Follow me.' Green resentfully led Enrique back to the cells.

In the jail behind the office, Enrique found the Strong brothers in two neighbouring cells. Enrique loathed the Strongs. This species of criminal was beneath him. They were dangerous idiots, but – he supposed – they had their uses.

The Strongs had drifted into Crow Valley. They had, rather stupidly, botched an ill-conceived stagecoach robbery. The Strongs were wanted for one thing or another all over Wyoming. They were looking at a long prison sentence, or even the noose. Despite their potentially miserable future, they were in high spirits when Enrique walked up to the iron bars.

'Looky here, Charlie! Enrique come to break us out!' Dwight Strong screeched.

The younger of the Strongs, Dwight was almost skeletally meagre. His greed for candy and cake had ruined his remaining teeth. Dwight's blackened smile, and shock of blond hair so thin it was nearly transparent, gave him a ghostly appearance. His almost perpetual shrieks of laughter only added to his banshee countenance.

Dwight was childishly mercurial. The slightest provocation could rouse his psychotic rage, or even his ecstatic delight. Were it not for the loyalty and guidance of his equally evil brother, Dwight would have been murdered or hung by now.

Physically and temperamentally, Charlie was a contrast to his brother Dwight. During his middle years, Charlie's own middle had swelled. His breeches struggled to contain his growing gut. Charlie's ruddy face had fattened, too. Age had yet to grey his black hair and moustache, and his dark eyes were bottomless wells of calculating ruthlessness.

'OK, Sheriff. Let them out.'

Green played along. He was hating every second of this – but he was desperate for the money. Enrique did not know nor care how Green would explain the Strongs' disappearance from his custody. The killer forced himself to feign gregariousness, shaking the Strongs' hands and trying not to grimace when they slapped his back.

Enrique led the Strongs to the town's livery, where he had arranged for horses to be waiting for the jailbreakers.

The assassin explained, 'There's plenty of cash in the saddlebags, boys. Weapons, too. You've been good to the boss, and he's rewarding you. But he needs you to do one more job.'

Charlie's ears pricked up like a wolf's. 'Anything, Enrique.'

Enrique paused. He had had to rescue the Strongs several times over the years. Enrique wondered if they were worthy of this strange assignment.

'I need you to set up a kidnapping.'

CHAPTER 1

From their crow's nest on the gentle hill overlooking Morriston, the Strong brothers spied their prey in the corral below. Charlie and Dwight Strong were accomplished criminals, but kidnap was a new challenge for them. Like circling hawks, they studied their quarry.

They had been instructed to spirit away Adam and Bob Connor. Adam and Bob, respectively eighteen and nineteen years old, were presently tending to their horses in the enclosure behind their father's house. The pastel colours of Monday's purple dusk were gradually darkening the grasslands, and the corral was a perfect picture of serenity. The Strongs could not decipher what the Connors were saying from this distance. Though the sounds which swam through the still, cool, sunset air were unintelligible, the Strongs could sense that the young men's voices were full of joy and playfulness.

'Looks like they're havin' a real nice time down there,' Dwight giggled.

'Sure does,' Charlie agreed, grinning callously. 'Let's put a stop to it.' Charlie felt a flicker of bitter resentment on seeing the Connors contentedly tending to their rides.

The Strongs' own childhood had not been quite as charmed.

They cantered down the hill towards the Connor house. Their residence was rather remote from Morriston, and Charlie was glad that there were no witnesses. During their crimes, the Strongs had never entertained the sentiments of compassion nor humanity. Charlie hoped that the Connors would not resist. He had been commanded not to harm them. Not much.

Adam and Bob were atop their mounts. They were not riding, exactly. Rather, they spiritedly walked the horses around the enclosure as they chatted. Adam and Bob worked with their father Eli in his general store. Pa was currently inside, dozing in his chair. The brothers enjoyed seeing to their rides, grooming them and mucking them out before they fixed their supper. They had lost Ma many years ago, so cooking and cleaning had become their chores.

'Who do you reckon that is?' Adam chirped. Morriston was a rural community dominated by farmers and ranchers. Strangers were not common, and the townsfolk welcomed travellers with polite caution. Nevertheless, the Connors were curious about the approaching riders. The two black dots on the hillside soon magnified into shadows. The strangers rode nearer and nearer.

'Don't say too much, Adam,' Bob warned. 'Let's just say Hi and leave them to it. They could be anyone.' Bob was the older and more cautious of the Connors. He was less boisterous and mischievous than Adam, yet fiercely protective of him.

As soon as the Strongs reached the corral fence, Adam rode over to greet them. With his light-brown hair and

11

slight frame, Adam was cherubic, or girlish even. It belied his brash, bold nature.

'Howdy,' he piped. Bob, though, was instantly suspicious. The porcine interloper and his spectral companion did not strike him as men of character.

'Howdy, boys,' Charlie responded. 'It's a grand evening. Come and have a ride with us.'

Eli had long warned his sons about invitations from strange men. 'No thanks, partner. We're just heading inside for some grub,' Adam responded, perturbed by the fat man's weird bidding.

The Strongs drew their Colts and cocked them.

'I'm not making a request,' snarled Charlie, to the music of Dwight's shrill snigger.

Within, Eli was startled from the comfort of his snooze by the report of a handgun blast. It was not unusual for weapons to be fired in the distance in this area, yet Eli immediately knew there was danger in the air. The feeling of peril magnified his senses. That gunshot originated from right outside, and in the cool, evening air he could smell the faint scent of gunpowder.

Springing from his chair, he ran to the window. Outside, the corral was empty. His sons and their mounts were absent, and he could hear the insistent gallop of fleeing horses. Acting with instinct and not calculation, he unlocked his gun cabinet. Eli seized his shotgun, which he rapidly loaded.

Eli darted outside. The sound of escaping hoofs had faded away into an eerie – yet electric – silence. He strolled over to the perimeter of the corral, the gravity of the situation slowly pressing on him. His sons had vanished.

Pacing the fence, his mind was a dizzy nest of scorpions. His sons were grown men, and they could come and go as they pleased, he told himself. There were no drops of blood and there was no damage. Though there were no physical signs of a fight, this did not relieve the rock of fear in Eli's breast.

Something winked at him from the grassy ground. He bent down to inspect the object: a bullet shell. The round was still warm when he fingered it. His sons had been unarmed, for Eli forbade them from carrying guns. The discarded bullet was the sign of an intruder.

Within the corral, something writhed in the grass, a cloth object animated by the gentle breeze. Eli ducked through the wires in the fence and walked over to the tiny garment. Picking it up, Eli found that it was a string tie – and an expensive one at that. Its black silk was smooth against his fingertips.

This odd discovery unnerved him, adding to his desperate fear. Where the heck were his sons? For a moment, Eli thought he heard something. It was not laughter exactly: rather, it sounded like a faraway, piercing howl. As Eli rode into town to the sheriff's office, he wondered if his own imagination was mocking him.

CHAPTER 2

It was typically a brief ride from his home to town – only a few miles. Galloping as the shadows began to magnify, Eli's troubled mind made the short journey seem almost endless. The sun had shrunk to but a thin, pink cinder on the horizon. Eli usually savoured the calm, refreshing, sundown air. Tonight, though, his nostrils were filled with the salty odour of his mount's perspiration, for he spurred his steed with punishing insistence. Eli gripped the reins with such intensity that his fingers reddened. The cruel tattoo of the hoofs on the spartan, dirt track was deafening.

At last, he reached town. Eli was relieved to see a light on in the sheriff's office.

Morriston had a sheriff of sorts: Frank Lee. Frank's main occupation was farming his homestead. With two grown-up sons, Frank had more time on his hands these days. He put his name forward to be the township's lawman, largely because nobody else wanted the job. There were punch-ups in the saloon, cattle thefts and other petty crimes. The townsfolk, though, were very private families. Serious crime was almost unknown.

14

The peacefulness of Morriston – at least compared to other lawless parts of Wyoming territory – was in part due to its benefactor, John Morris. Morris was a mysterious blend of political leader, business investor and philanthropist. He owned his own ranch, and shares in many of the farms around Morriston – including Frank's. Morris' ancestors, some of the earliest settlers in Wyoming, founded the settlement. Morris paid for the school, the church, and even Frank's own wages. A recluse, Morris would appear at Christmas and the Summer carnival. Something of a benign dictator, Morris ran his town from afar. Individual townsfolk – Frank included – seldom met him in person.

Early on Monday evening, Frank had been busying himself in the sheriff's office. The building was a simple construction with a single jail cell that Frank had never used. He was a snowy-haired, bespectacled man who had the manner of a gentle grandfather (which he was). Going through the sheriff's thin correspondence was something of a hobby for him, an escape from the brood of screaming babies back home. Frank adored his grandchildren, but enjoyed his brief respites in the lawman's bureau.

Eli knocked on his door, then burst in before Frank could open it.

'Sheriff,' Eli blurted with breathless insistence. 'May I come in? Something's happened to my boys.'

Eli, while his sons had grown into men, had retained his lean frame. His thin, black hair and moustache were lightly dusted with the grey of his years. Tonight though, Frank noted, Eli's customarily keen, brown eyes were sunken. His shirt was glued to his flesh by patches of

15

dripping sweat. Eli was wheezing desperately.

'Step inside,' Frank answered. Frank was concerned for Eli, but had to restrain his sigh. Eli's agitation suggested that his problem was not going to be easy to resolve. 'How can I help?'

'My boys,' panted Eli. 'They were in the corral out back. I was inside, sleeping. There was a gunshot and I ran out back. My boys were gone, along with their rides. Far off, I heard some horses riding away mighty fast. I found this bullet shell on the ground, and this string tie.'

Eli retrieved the clues from his pocket, and showed them to the sheriff. 'What the heck is going on, Frank? My boys have vanished.'

Frank needed to think quickly. He had no idea how he would deal with a kidnap.

'Did they say anything about going for a ride, or venturing off some place?'

Eli shuddered with frustration. He was fearful that the sheriff would not know what to do. The brow of Frank's kind face was furrowed. He was speaking hesitantly, as if improvising his responses.

'No, Frank. Nothing. It's not like my boys to just disappear. Something's happened, Frank. I've just got this real bad feeling in my guts.'

The repellent, grey gloom of night was now filling the air outside. Frank knew that Eli was looking to him for leadership. With the skies darkening, Frank had to decide fast. Frank hoped that his meek decision-making did not show in his voice.

He fixed Eli with what Frank hoped was an authoritative stare. The storekeeper had a haunted aspect to him. His skin seemed to have greyed and the man appeared to have aged considerably in only a few hours.

'Mr Connor – I know you have raised two good boys. There's a story behind all this, and we'll find it out soon enough. But I'm sending you home. There ain't no sense in sending a posse out on the plains after nightfall. Hang onto those items. Call on me again on the morrow.' Frank hoped that he sounded masterful.

'Yes, Sheriff. See you in the mornin'.' Eli turned away. Once again, his infuriation was expressed in the briefest of shudders. Just before setting off, though, he glowered powerfully at Frank. The sheriff detected an inner rage and resolve in that brief glance. He did not like the look of it.

Emotionally shattered, Eli trudged back home. This time, he did not gallop. There seemed little point. Though the menacing black of nightfall was now gluttonously swallowing the sunlight, Eli instinctively knew the way back. Frank was a good and decent man, he thought to himself. However, the sheriff was not equipped for whatever was happening.

The house was deathly silent without his sons. Once inside, the quiet and emptiness only worsened Eli's incessant thoughts. The same horrific visions played over and over in his mind's eye. Eli did not even contemplate eating or sleeping. He entered his own bedroom where he kept his gun cabinet.

He withdrew a rifle and began to wipe away the rust with a wire brush. The carbine was long disused. The metal screeched as Eli made thorough strokes with the metallic mesh. Though speckles of brown rust sprayed into his eyes, he did not flinch.

Eli never thought that he would have to kill again.

CHAPTER 3

Eli had been a drover in his youth. The long cattle drives, while testing on his energies, had been valuable opportunities to save money. A cowpuncher earned dollars nearly twenty-four hours a day. Out on the plains, there was nothing to waste your money on. Eli never recklessly squandered his cash on whiskey or worse. He put his money in the bank. Years of saving and a modest loan from an investor, finally enabled Eli to buy his own general store in Morriston.

That was the tapestry of lies which Eli had weaved to protect his sons. It was a fiction that he had supported for nearly twenty years.

He had, in truth, been a hired gun and a bounty hunter. Eli had been a successful plodder, if not material for campfire legends. He had been a stickler who could finish the job, and not a vain quick-draw man boasting down at the saloon.

As a young man, Eli had learned how to follow a trail. This meant human intelligence as much as an eye for hoofprints, or broken blades of grass. When he determined to capture (or kill) a miscreant, Eli acted with

18

endless perseverance and patience. He would ride from settlement to settlement for weeks and weeks until he found his man.

Eli was not always fortunate. His quarries – who were never the amiable sort – would sometimes be slain by their own enemies. On other occasions, one of Eli's mercenary contemporaries might accost or eliminate the target before Eli had the opportunity.

Such disappointments never deflated Eli. Though he was a skilled marksman, his great strength was not his dexterity as a gunman. His true edge was his tenacity. When he was bested in a manhunt by one of his fellow professionals, Eli simply set his sights on his next game and soldiered on.

There was one nugget of veracity in the fantasy which Eli had created for Adam and Bob. For an individual who earned his income by beating up or shooting wanted criminals for the price on their neck, Eli was very temperate. After riding into town with a man in handcuffs, Eli would pay for a hot bath, a steak, and then go straight to bed. His bounties were banked immediately.

He never dwelled on the violence he inflicted. In his core, Eli was not a cruel man. He never utilised excess brutality. Perhaps it was this spark of decency that drew Cassie to him.

She was a Morriston girl. Eli was passing through town, obsessively tracking his prey. Cassie was a waitress in the Morriston Café. The two began chatting while she served Eli his coffee. Golden-haired with blue eyes as beautiful and hypnotic as gemstones, Cassie's beauty was beguiling. It was more than her physical loveliness that struck Eli, though. He was charmed by the ease with which they talked. Eli's years of manhunting had been lonesome, and he had indeed grown into a curmudgeon. Comely Cassie, though, had instantly magicked away Eli's solitary surliness.

A few days later, Eli took a job as a farmhand. He and Cassie began stepping out together. Eli, once so single-minded, could not even remember the name of the man he had been tracking. He now comprehended what they were talking about in love songs and dime-store novels.

Indeed, he could scarcely recognise his own reflection in the mirror. He found himself almost perpetually smiling. Sauntering energetically down the main street, Eli – once so wary of strangers – greeted passers-by with a friendly 'Howdy.'

His way of life was transformed over the next months. Eli wed Cassie, and she gifted him two sons. He withdrew all his savings, and risked it on a business: his general store.

The following ten years were so blissful that – to Eli – it seemed like a century of delight. Retrospectively, Eli wondered how he had possibly lived through so much happiness in such a short time. Working in his store and coming home to his boys and beautiful wife every day made him feel wealthy in a way beyond earthly monies.

So powerful was Eli's love that, even when Cassie succumbed to cholera, he considered himself unimaginably fortunate to have shared so much time with her. Though saddened, Eli needed to be strong for his sons. He saved his weeping for his blackest, private hours. Even after ten years as a widower, Eli still felt that there were teardrops in him that were yet to fall.

*

Monday night had been wakeful, and Eli had not even attempted to sleep. He had busied himself by loading his saddle bags and cleaning his rifle and pistols. Eli also studied maps and newspapers. Before his sons' abduction – for Eli was certain that his boys had been coerced – he had been beginning to feel the aches and sluggishness of creeping old age. Eli had an audible crack in his hip, and at times the mere act of stiffly standing up was an irritation.

These physical trifles were banished from his mind. Eli was remembering, now: not facts, but instincts. A hunter once more, Eli's motivation was deeper than the urge to win a few dollars in bounty. His sons were in danger, and Eli could feel their fear as palpably as if he were the one in peril. Losing Adam and Bob – his own bloodline, and the only part of Cassie still living – would be akin to losing limbs.

Eli would set off at dawn. Though the night seemed endless, Eli knew that he would need daylight to follow the trail. Sheriff Lee, and his equally kind yet ineffectual deputies, would debate the problem all day. With every minute, Adam and Bob were carried off further and further away. Eli had no time for the sheriff's useless good intentions.

The sun seemed reluctant as it finally peered over the grasslands. The slim shard of gloomy illumination slowly lifted the night's murky threat, though the grey light of morning looked equally ominous.

So be it, thought Eli. There will be danger ahead, but my sons need me.

Before riding off into the prairie, Eli put a sign up in his shop window.

'Closed until further notice.'

Eli's customers would have to do without cans of beans. He was ready to slice away the flesh of his sons' abductors inch by bloody inch.

CHAPTER 4

Frank watched Eli retreating to his house. The sheriff, though he was ostensibly the law in Morriston, somehow felt that he had erred. Frank was genuinely disconcerted that Adam and Bob seemed to have disappeared.

Should I have raised a posse? he asked himself. Ought I have saddled up and ridden out all by myself? Is that what a sheriff does?

It doesn't matter if you're right or wrong, Frank told himself. But you have to decide.

Eli had seemed very angry before the sheriff had sent him away. Frank wondered whether this time he was wrong. The sheriff sighed, envying the murmuring laughter coming from the saloon. He was tempted to join the drinkers in the bar, but given the seriousness of Eli's predicament, he did not want to be seen there.

Instead, Frank closed the office door after him and returned to his chair. He randomly picked a sheet of paper, if only to give himself something to stare at. He pulled back his desk drawer, where his whiskey bottle rolled and clinked. Frank poured himself a slug. The sheriff often joked to himself that the liquor was for emergencies only, but the bottle was half empty.

Emergencies only? Frank asked himself mockingly. When was the last time you dealt with an emergency? His rhetorical question, and Eli's visit, triggered a long-dormant memory. The last time Morriston experienced a serious incident was when Eli first arrived in town. Frank took a burning sip from his glass as he remembered.

Eli had been the town's shopkeeper some twenty years. He and his sons were familiar and popular faces. Adam and Bob had been born in Morriston. In such an interdependent community, though, Eli was a comparative newcomer.

The sun had been radiating wave after hazy wave of cruel heat that day. Frank had been called away from his farm to deal with a belligerent drunk. The booze-hound was a stranger to Morriston. He had plenty of cash in his pocket, and had been imbibing heavily for days. The townsfolk tended to take a courteous step back from unknown faces. The barman had served the stranger politely, but eventually the outsider began harassing the locals and breaking furniture.

Frank had been younger and leaner back then. He was but an occasional deputy, and not experienced in matters of keeping the peace. Frank still recalled taking hesitant steps up to the saloon bar, the suffocating heat haze – or perhaps his own fear – an invisible force seemingly driving him back. He almost wished some unseen magnetism would suck him away.

Entering the drinking den, Frank found it empty but for a frightened barman and the intoxicated stranger; he was leaning against the bar, barely able to stand. The outsider was expounding an unintelligible, mumbled monologue to which the nervous bartender was nodding politely. As Frank approached the stranger, his handcuffs jangled. The deputy hoped that his own nerves were not making the manacles clink.

'Morning, partner,' Frank squeaked, as cheerfully as he could. Frank hoped that the drunkard would yield without an altercation. His gorge as dry as sand, Frank painstakingly and self-consciously swallowed. He could sense the stranger watching his Adam's apple rise and fall. 'Mind if I have a word?'

Swaggering yet staggering, the drunk turned to face Frank. He could hardly stand. The stranger paused arrogantly, eyeing the deputy contemptuously before responding.

'Sure thing, deputy,' the drunk hissed. His rotten breath struck Frank like the gas from a cesspit. Frank was already nervous, but the air of sickening decay from the stranger made Frank want to vomit. The drunk was built like a hog, but was not as clean. His clothes and flesh were unwashed to the point that they seemed to mix into a single, smelly crust. Every detail and aspect of the man was repellent.

'How about you call it a day, buddy? It's not noon and you've had a couple of beers already.'

The stranger made a show of looking over his shoulders and around the bar. Broken chairs and tables – no doubt shattered by the intruder himself – were scattered around the saloon.

'What makes you say that, deputy?' the stranger spat sarcastically. The drunk's silly barb irked Frank, and he could sense that a cordial approach was ineffectual. Frank reached for his handcuffs, but before he even lay a finger on them, the stranger swung one of his trotters into the deputy's forehead. Frank recoiled in pain and shock. Though dizzied and bruised, Frank was about to try and accost the drunk once again when the swine drew his Remington. Though the stranger could not hold the weapon steady, this did not allay Frank's fears.

The report of the gunshot nearly arrested Frank's heartbeat. Even when the hog collapsed, blood running from his snout, Frank could not quite comprehend what had taken place.

Eli lowered the smoking revolver in his right hand, and placed a reassuring palm on Frank's shoulder with the other. The deputy jolted.

When Eli explained the situation, he did not come across as brash nor daring (brave though he was). For a bounty hunter, Eli was very matter-of-fact and reserved. His coal-black hair and angular features were undoubtedly handsome, but he had the manner of a bank manager.

Back in the sheriff's office, Eli showed Frank and the then-sheriff a wanted poster: Scott Glenn, $100 reward, dead or alive. The man pictured did indeed resemble the drunkard. The sheriff did not usually appreciate bounty hunter characters, but in this instance, he did not take issue.

Eli declined Frank's offer of a drink, asking instead where he could eat a good steak.

'Morriston Café,' Frank advised. 'Cassie'll take care of you.'

Cassie took very good care of Eli indeed, for two weeks

later, Cassie and Eli were stepping out together. Frank found Eli some work on his farm. The taciturn mercenary was now so in love that he even forgot to claim the hundred-dollar bounty. John Morris' men discreetly disposed of Scott Glenn's remains.

Frank was startled from his reminiscence by a powerful rap on his office door. 'What now?' he asked the empty air languidly. Opening the door, Frank was jolted from his lethargy when he saw who his visitor was.

CHAPTER 5

Adam and Bob complied when the song of Charlie's revolver played stridently in their ears. Terrified, they obediently left their corral and followed the Strongs out onto the plains. Charlie and Dwight flanked the Connors, each of the Strongs riding with one hand on his reins and the other on his Colt.

The Strongs spurred their mounts with cruel firmness. Riding in a reckless gallop, the four sped away on what may have been a random course. The Connors were too frightened to pay too much attention to the direction. Adam and Bob were not certain whether the devastating drum in their ears was hoofbeats or heartbeats.

They rode for miles. It was disorientating to gallop so blindly. Bob did not know how the Strongs could tell which way they were riding, if they knew where they were going at all.

Soon, only the pinpricks of starlight in the murky skies illuminated them. When the obscurity was so black that they could not see their hands on the reins, Charlie halted his criminal convoy.

By then, their mounts were slippery with perspiration.

It was careless to punish a horse so, but the Strongs did not seem to know, nor care. As the animals exhaled breathily, the Strongs dismounted.

'Get down, boys,' Charlie commanded. 'Unpack our saddle bags and start a fire.'

'Now wait just a minute, mister,' Adam interjected. Scared though he was, fear had not quelled Adam's brashness nor innate cheek. 'Where the heck are you taking us? What's going on?'

The impact of Dwight's gun handle on Adam's forehead stung, and drew blood. Adam was on his knees, lines of blood from his gash entwining with streaks of tears from his eyes, before he realized what had happened. He fought to restrain his sobs, while a wave of impotent rage swelled within him. Dwight's surreal shrieks of laughter only magnified Adam's anger.

As Adam sprang to his feet ready to pummel Dwight, Bob bear-hugged him from behind, holding him back. Bob needed to tighten his arms forcefully as Adam writhed in fury.

The Strongs laughed in chorus.

'You got some fight, boy. I like that. Don't go too crazy, now, 'cause Dwight and me got plenty of fight, too.'

To emphasise his point, Charlie lashed out with his own Colt, striking Bob on his head. The bite of Charlie's pistol-whip repulsed Bob, forcing him to release Adam. Bob wiped the blood away, streaking the back of his hand. Painful though it was, Bob did not yelp nor whimper. Instead, he fixed Charlie with a penetrating stare. Charlie did not like that disdainful glower.

'Now get to work!' he barked.

As the Connors unpacked, their heads stinging, the

Strongs conjured a quart of whiskey from somewhere. Bob tried to eavesdrop as he set up camp, but it was futile. It was as though the Strong brothers had been each other's companions for so long that they had developed a unique language that only the two of them could understand. They appeared to use distinctive slang that only they could comprehend. Watered by whiskey, they giggled at private jokes that were only funny to them.

Adam unpacked as if in an angry trance. His body was moving, apparently in accordance with Charlie's command. Mentally, Adam was imagining the violent ends to which he could deliver his captors.

The distant orchestra of crickets and the lambent crackle of the campfire would have been pleasing in other circumstances. When the unpacking was complete, the Strongs commanded their abductees to sit down. As the four sat around the flames, its flickering red light only deepened the hellishness of the situation. The Strongs had bidden their new wards to warm some oats over the fire. Adam had at first defiantly refused to eat, but Charlie had insisted. The Strongs devoured their porridge, whereas the Connors had to compel themselves to swallow the lukewarm lumps.

Curiously, Bob noted, the Strongs had brought along four metal serving trays. The kidnap was not impulsive. It had been planned.

After the thin meal, the Connors shivered as Charlie rose and strolled over to them. Charlie cast his shadow over them, and they trembled.

'You might as well sleep, boys. Me and Dwight'll be watching you, so don't try nothing. It's going to be a long ride tomorrow.'

Charlie fetched four bedrolls from his saddlebags. Once again, Bob noted, the Strongs had come packed for four. Dwight took the first watch, as Charlie and the Connors bedded down. Bob was exhausted – as much from his relentless fear as from the strains of the violent ride – yet slumber was impossible. During the night, Bob turned over and over. Adam was similarly restless.

Dwight's sinister vigil did nothing to relax him. He sat upright all night, silently watching over his charges like a gargoyle. Bob was still wakeful when Charlie took the watch. Pallid though Dwight came across, he always seemed to be bursting with childish energy. Charlie, however, wheezed and sighed as he laboriously rose from his bedroll. Indeed, Bob thought he heard Charlie snoozing when he was supposed to be guarding them – though Bob dared not attempt to flee.

Bob remained wakeful when faraway birdsong began to chirp, and the secretive darkness surrendered to grey dawn. He allowed himself to watch the fiery sun peep over the horizon. The sun seemed to be benevolently spying on the vast plains below. It made Bob feel oddly envious, for his own guardians were not as benign.

It did not take much to rouse a needle of mercurial energy such as Dwight. When he sensed the gentle sunlight on his flesh, he awoke with a start. Immediately, his shrill sniggers began.

'Wakey wakey, boys. Now you get goin' and warm us up some coffee. Got a lot to do today, boys,' he giggled. Dwight did not berate Charlie for sleeping through his watch. Charlie appeared to be the senior partner in their relationship.

Still fatigued, the Connors obediently rose and relit the

fire. Warming the kettle, the brothers were slightly chilled in the fresh morning air. Adam and Bob tried not to look when the Strongs began cleaning two rifles. Adam, though, in dread as much as curiosity, broke his silence.

'What are you doing with those there rifles, Mr Strong?'

Charlie grinned like a toad, and winked at Adam.

'You'll see, boy.'

CHAPTER 6

Eli had tucked the silk tie into the inside pocket of his jacket. It was his only clue and he had an idea where to start. Eli was riding south to Bridgwater, a settlement some ten miles from Morriston. There was a fine tailor in Bridgwater, and Eli was keen to see what he knew of the garment.

To the East, the sun laboriously climbed into the heavens. The sight of dawn over the prairie awed Eli at other times. Now, the plains yawned before him like an endless green sea. That ocean of grassland was calm now, and deathly quiet, but Eli wondered what horrors the prairie concealed.

Desperate though Eli was, he was mindful to moderate the pace of his ride. His steed would need its energy, as would he. Eli licked his lips in a futile effort to moisten them. His maw was as dry as a desiccated bone. Eli had not eaten, slept, nor even drank a glass of water. Pure adrenalin carried him along.

Bridgwater loomed in the distance. Though but a few miles away, so agitated was Eli that the minutes passed like hours. He could see early risers setting off to work, and a handful of passers-by. Eli was determined to question the tailor: if his shop was shut, Eli would drag the man from his bed.

Bridgwater was comparatively monied for that part of Wyoming. The town boasted an expensive restaurant, a plush hotel and a photography studio. Eli had always found Bridgwater to be a little uppity and stuck up. As he halted his horse and tied it to a rail, he tried to ignore the inquisitive – and disdainful – glances he was receiving. Eli had no time for gawkers, and walked straight to the tailor's.

He found that, though early, the tailor was at his premises. Eli had not seen Seth Fritz since his wedding to Cassie. Fritz had fitted up almost every man in the region with his wedding suit. He was a wiry, awkward individual. Fritz would rather have sat in a dark room and sewed than sipped a beer in the sunshine, and he was indeed so pale he looked sickly. Shy misfit though he was, Fritz was an expert craftsman.

As Eli entered the shop, Fritz was at his table, tending to a garment. Eli noted Fritz's, prehensile fingers, which were as long and dextrous as a tarantula's legs. Before Eli could speak, Fritz looked up and addressed him.

'Mr Connor. I don't think I've seen you for twenty years. How can I be of assistance?' Oddball though he was, Fritz's mind was sharper than one of his needles. The tailor must have been much older than Eli, but Fritz was unfading in the way that a ghost never ages.

Eli was taken aback, but would not let it show. He approached Fritz and showed him the silk tie.

'I'd be interested to know what you can tell me about this.'

Fritz laughed knowingly. 'You wouldn't be calling at this hour to buy some new socks,' he smirked. The tailor took the tie, and rubbed it between his thumb and forefinger.

'This is one of my garments, Mr Connor. A few days ago, two men called in to be fitted up for wedding suits. They seemed to be . . . rough diamonds, shall we say? But they paid cash up front for two suits – and expensive ones at that. I supplied two silk ties with those suits.' Fritz indicated the tie in his hand. 'This was one of them,' he said with certainty.

'These two rough diamonds,' Eli implored. 'Describe them.' He hoped that his despair was not audible in his voice.

Fritz leaned back in his chair, eyeing Eli suspiciously. He lay down his needle and made an arch with his elongated fingers and thumb. It was as though Fritz had intuited Eli's desperation, and was drawing haughty pleasure from taking pause.

'What's this all about, Mr Connor? You are not a lawman, although I am aware of your . . . past.'

Eli resented Fritz's accusatory tone, but did not rise to the provocation. Fritz was not a pack animal. Though he spoke without emotion, his words were irksome nonetheless.

'My sons . . . last night, I heard a gunshot. When I went outside, my boys – and their rides – had vanished. I found the silk tie discarded in my corral. I'm certain my sons have been kidnapped.'

Fritz nodded. It was as if he were trying – yet failing – to convey compassion.

'There were two men. They said their names were

Charlie and Dwight Strong. Brothers. Charlie was a rotund fellow – black hair, black moustache. He did all the talking. Dwight was thin and grey-skinned. Blond in an ashen sort of way. Dwight did not talk much. I think he may have been a simpleton. He giggled almost nonstop.'

Fritz rose from his chair, and seemed to be eyeballing Eli. Eli would have found him threatening were it not for Fritz's pipe-cleaner physique.

'I think that tie was discarded on purpose, Mr Connor. The ties cost over a hundred dollars each. Not the sort of thing you would misplace accidentally. Somebody is trying to tell you something.'

Taking in Fritz's counsel, Eli glanced around the tailor's store. Mannequins lined the walls, each one with different absences of limbs or members. There seemed to be no pattern to how these human-sized dolls were dressed (or undressed). Various tables were strewn with sheets of cloth or half-finished garments. Unkempt though it appeared to him, Eli did not doubt that Fritz ordered his things with a sophistication lost on onlookers.

'Thank you, Mr Fritz. You've been very helpful. But I do have one more question. This wedding – did the Strong brothers say where it was?'

'They said it would be in Beulah. Not far from here.'

Eli nodded to show his appreciation. Fritz was not the handshake type, and Eli weirdly feared that he might crush Fritz's fragile digits under his own grip. Eli left without another word. Exiting the premises, he could feel the tailor's creepy gaze on the back of his head.

Eli mounted and rode off, glad to leave Fritz behind. His next destination would be no less uncomfortable, though, for Beulah was a ghost town.

CHAPTER 7

Fritz watched Eli riding away. His stern face – as white and firm as marble – showed no emotion. Inwardly, though, Fritz was pleased to see this particular chess piece advancing. Fritz hoped that this pawn would get as far away from him as possible.

He returned to his sewing. Fritz enjoyed working this early, for it meant – usually – that he could tailor without interruption. Though his business depended on delighting his customers, Fritz was a misanthrope. Were it not for his craftsmanship, his patrons would have tired of his severe and blunt manner long ago.

Fritz had an eye for detail. He sewed the garment on his table stitch by painstaking stitch. When he finished, the fine jacket he was creating would be immaculate. The tailor lost himself in his art, concentrating on nothing but the strokes of his needle. Fritz well knew the price of the slightest slip, for his one and only error had made him beholden to his master.

He had learned his craft from his father. Even as a child, Fritz had not gotten on well with other boys. Fritz could not fathom the appeal of their silly games, and their foolish fairy tales. He felt himself cleverer, superior. His childhood peers had never warmed to him, and – with no siblings – Fritz had long been a solitary man.

His parents had been very different. While they taught him skilfully, they were also warm, gregarious people. They despaired of his rude haughtiness, often pushing him to mix with other boys. Of course, when Fritz grew into a man, he was cheeriest working hour after hour. He was hardly a magnet for the ladies. His parents were gladdened by the productivity of their son, but concerned for his future happiness. Fritz's mother and father, with the kindest intentions, made a terrible error. They arranged his marriage.

'Now she's a lovely girl, Seth,' they urged. 'You're gonna love her. You're a young man. We can't have you locked up in the shop every hour.' Fritz still recalled these portentous words, and how he irked at them. He tried to resist. While his parents had always endured his retiring ways, on this matter, they would not yield.

Soon enough, Fritz, his new bride Abigail, and his parents were living together. The tailor's shop had always been prosperous, and the Fritzes lived in a fine, brick house just outside of town. Abigail's girlfriends envied the affluence she had married into. After a few weeks, Abigail was not so certain.

Had Fritz been more of an extrovert, he would have hurled pots and pans, and broken household artefacts on a nightly basis. This was not his way, though. Even though his bank account was bulging, and he shared his bed with a beautiful, young woman every night, Fritz seethed and sulked. Abigail was a kindly and dedicated wife, but this

was lost on Fritz. He could not bear her insufferable pleas-
antries, and batted her hand away when she walked her
fingers up his naked flesh at night.

When Fritz's mother and father finally passed away,
Fritz knew that his moment had come.

It was only the generosity and warmth of Fritz's parents
that sustained Abigail during her loveless partnership.
Without them, Fritz's coldness and indifference saddened
her. After a time, her soul sickened. She trudged around
the house tending to the housework absent-mindedly.
The stoniness of her husband crushed her.

While he always seemed aloof, Fritz was in fact watching Abigail from afar, waiting for her to slip. He was not
totally devoid of feeling, for Fritz was gifted with bound-
less spite and cruelty. Abigail had developed a taste for a
glass of wine, or three, every evening. She had once been
only an occasional drinker, but Abigail had grown desperate for something to mask her bleak misery. Fritz did
nothing to discourage this. Indeed, he made sure that his
wine cellar was stocked with excellent vintages from
California and South America.

Abigail had given up on asking after Fritz, so she did
not realize that he had started descending to the cellar
every night. There, drop by drop, he tainted the wines
with arsenic. He had stomached Abigail's galling presence for too many years.

This was Fritz's blunder. Not his decision to murder
Abigail, but getting caught.

Fritz believed that the poison would not be detectable.
When the undertakers took the body away, he blamed his
wife's ill health and weakness for strong drink.

'Excuse me if I do not weep,' he had told the funeral

men. 'I do not wear my heart on my sleeve.'

The tailor was proud of his crafty coup, but he was soon to understand that another man was slyer still.

John Morris, while based in his ranch outside Morriston, had spun a spider-web of influence. He owned businesses all over the region, including the undertaker's in Bridgwater. Morris was not suspicious of Abigail's demise. In fact, he clandestinely arranged for a doctor to examine in depth every single corpse which passed through the funeral home. Morris' intrusions occasionally found black secrets. When the rancher learned that Abigail showed signs of arsenic poisoning, he was very discreet.

The day that Morris appeared at Fritz's door, he was terrified. Even for one as reserved as Fritz, he physically trembled when Morris materialised. He knew that this visit portended trouble.

Morris was nearly seven foot tall. His greyed hair descended to his shoulders, but Morris did not come across as an old man. He reminded Morris of a totem pole that had stood for centuries.

The rancher had taken Fritz into the private room behind his shop. There, Morris had explained. The rancher had not embellished nor threatened.

'Mr Fritz,' he had begun. Though Morris spoke in a voice as coarse as gravel, he was unfailingly polite. 'It has come to my attention that Abigail was poisoned. What do you know about that?'

Fritz had not answered. His trembling silence was confession enough. Morris had laughed in an understanding way.

'I see, Mr Fritz. I see. Well, I'm not the law in these

parts. Not officially. I'm happy to respect your privacy. And I hope you'll appreciate my favour.'

Gulping, Fritz had nodded frantically.

'Good. I'll be dropping in some time.'

In the following years, Fritz did not see Morris again, although the rancher became his best customer. Morris did not return until a few days ago.

Shortly after Eli left for Beulah, Fritz sensed a shadow fall over him as somebody else entered his shop. The tailor did not need to look up. He knew who it was.

'Did you tell Eli what I told you to tell him?' asked Morris.

'Yes,' pipped Fritz.

'Good.'

CHAPTER 8

The Strongs were wandering guns for hire – armed odd-job men. They would assassinate somebody, or thieve something, and then take off for the plains. Hardly out-doorsmen, they found their way on the grasslands by reckless trial-and-error. Often, they would be out on the prairie for weeks at a time.

If we don't know where the heck we are, they reasoned, the lawmen surely won't.

Charlie and Dwight were finding this particular outing to be highly enjoyable. They did not have to cook nor wash up. Their paymaster had something special in mind for the boys, so they had to keep them safe – or alive, at least. That said, the Connors could provide them with some company, and sport.

The party of fugitives was loosely wandering Eastwards. The trek was taking hours and hours, and Charlie occa-sionally stopped the convoy. During these breaks, the Strongs would run little lessons in lawlessness. Charlie and Dwight would teach their charges some knife-fight-ing, quick-drawing, or rifle shooting. The Strongs could sense the boys' apprehension and reluctance, but they cooperated.

Charlie found Bob to be the more studied and careful brother. Charlie suspected a mixture of averseness, home-sickness and fear in Bob. For all of Bob's reserve, though, Charlie found that Bob was his favourite. He could see similarities with himself. Like so many eldest siblings, Charlie and Bob were the more calculating and measured brothers.

Charlie also valued Bob's intelligence. Of course, he also appreciated Adam's clumsy zeal. However, Bob listened attentively to Charlie's instruction. Charlie felt that Bob was learning something.

At one point, Charlie spied a colony of rabbits frolicking ahead of them, and stopped the riding party. He did not want to startle the creatures: they would give him and his charges some amusement. The animals were barely black spots in the distance. After a lifetime of scanning the horizon for threats, though, Charlie's eyesight was outstanding.

'OK, y'all – let's dismount,' Charlie ordered. He approached Adam and lay an ostensibly fatherly hand on the youngster's shoulder.

This made Bob want to scowl, but he controlled himself. Though his younger brother was the bolder and gutsier sibling, Bob nevertheless felt an iron protective-ness towards Adam. The two had had no opportunity to converse privately since joining the Strongs. Bob knew that their father would be an emotional wreck.

'Young Adam.' Charlie enjoyed portraying the role of a teacher. 'You see them rabbits yonder? Let me see you bag one.'

He loaded his single shot rifle, aimed, and missed. Never one to be discouraged, Adam took aim and fired once again. Adam missed a second time, but shot a rabbit on his third attempt. The tiny beast flopped lifelessly in the distance.

Dwight sniggered his approval, and Charlie turned his attention to Bob.

'Your turn now, Bob. Let's see how Mr Safe Pair of Hands manages it.' Charlie smiled fondly, and Bob smiled back. Bob had noted that Charlie seemed particularly keen on him. It sickened Bob, but he played along.

Bob expertly loaded the rifle, pressed its butt against his shoulder, and peered down the sights. The rifle sight was never an exact guide, but Bob had learned where the sight needed to be in relation to the target. He squeezed the trigger. The carbine recoiled, but Bob's grip on the weapon was masterful. Inhaling the smoky wisps of carbonite, Bob saw that he had felled a rabbit.

The Strongs whooped and cheered. Bob reddened, a little embarrassed despite himself. Charlie could not resist commenting.

'Young Adam – he's the crazy one. He'll shoot and shoot 'til he hits his mark. But Bob – he's like a buzzard. He hovers and waits – and strikes! Bang! One shot – it's all over. I'm glad you're riding with us, boys. We will make one heck of a team.'

Dwight reacted with more cheer. Bob felt flattered – but caught himself. He knew that Charlie's words were insincere. Charlie had something in mind for the Connors, and his glib compliments were merely to indulge his new wards.

'Now then,' Charlie continued. 'Dwight – show us how

a Strong bags a couple of rabbits.'

Bob had been trying to keep away from Dwight, so far as he could. He found Dwight to be a monstrous and repellent spectre. Dwight was skeletal and ghostly pale. His almost constant banshee cackle literally made Bob shudder.

In moments, Dwight had loaded and fired the single shot rifle some dozen times. Bob lost count, so swift was Dwight's handling of the carbine. He was not unlike a machine: a clockwork man whose spinning cogs served to operate a weapon. Dwight did not appear to be taking careful aim. Rather, he seemed to innately predict where the rabbits would run. Dwight turned some twelve of the animals into small, bloody explosions. Bob did not think he had missed once, but Dwight was so devilishly fast it was impossible to say.

Dwight giggled proudly.

Charlie turned to Bob. 'See those dead rabbits, Bob? That's what the Strongs do to anybody gets in our way.'

Charlie cupped Bob's chin in his hand in a gesture disgusting in its intimacy. 'I'll make an outlaw of you yet, Bob.'

CHAPTER 9

Riding to Beulah, Eli could not shake off his inkling that he was being watched. It was something more than the eerie stare of that sinister tailor. During his first career, Eli sometimes found that his prey attempted to reverse the game, slyly stalking him. They thought they were smart, but Eli was always the more cunning. Such an expert man-hunter and tracker was Eli that he had a feel for such situations. The prickling in his breast warned him, and it was never long before Eli confronted his quarry in a deadly showdown.

Though it had been many years, Eli again felt that familiar prickle alerting him. The sun was powerfully radiant, but it was not the heat making thick marbles of perspiration run down his brow. The salty sweat was viscous in his mouth. Somebody is out there, Eli realized.

That he was being directed to Beulah was another warning. Only a short ride from Bridgwater, Eli could see the black shapes of the abandoned settlement sitting on the horizon. Once a lively, if little, township, Beulah had been long deserted. Cholera had slain many of its denizens, and the survivors had walked away. Nobody but phantoms got married in Beulah.

Drawing into the ghost town, Eli halted his roan. Before dismounting, he looked around swiftly. The wooden buildings were now wrecks, overgrown by weeds and grass. Small though Beulah was, it had once boasted a fine, stone church. The town had been a popular site for weddings. Even the church was now in a state of collapse. Its roof, windows and doors had all gone. Apparently empty of humans, this graveyard of a town could be a hiding place. Eli drew his Colt in readiness.

He stepped down from his mount. Eli was not frightened. Rather, his senses were sharpened and wakeful. There was a slightest breeze, and the thin grass on the ground danced to its whistling melody. It did nothing to cool Eli's flushed flesh.

Some huntsman's instinct urged him to start with the church. Those ne'er-do-wells who had visited Fritz were playing a game with him. Eli knew that this reconnaissance could be a fool's errand – or worse, a trap.

Entering the church, Eli felt oddly like a medieval knight braving a fortress. The door of the church had long gone. Within, the pews and altar remained. They had decayed considerably, and the weeds which had invaded through the floor, were clawing the wooden interior back to the earth. It was surreal to be wading through grass which grew to his ankles. Eli half-expected a priest or choirboy to break the quiet.

He strode down the aisle to the back of the church. Perhaps because his sense of danger had magnified his hearing, the sound of the grass brushing against his boots was akin to the report of a bullwhip. Eli noted that there were still bibles and hymn books on some of the benches. This was once a place of serenity and peace, he thought.

Presently, though, the air was electric with peril.

Outside, John Morris tied his reins to a building some distance from the church. He had had to be vigilant while following Eli. Morris remembered Eli from before his metamorphosis into the local, affable storekeeper. Even before Eli had arrived in Morriston, Morris knew Eli by reputation. The rancher's business dealings had not always been within the letter and spirit of the law. Morris' men had been accosted by Eli several times. He knew how expert Eli was, and so today's pursuit had been especially careful.

He tiptoed through Beulah's wrecked houses until he was close to the church. Peering around the side of an old building, Morris could see Eli investigating, through the unframed windows. The rancher would watch for now. Eli was a thorough man. Soon, Morris hoped, Eli would find the little surprise he had left in there for him.

Finding nothing of note in the pews nor the back of the church, Eli walked up to the altar. On the pulpit, Eli found a single hymn sheet. The words to Pure Heart. It was baffling that, in this desolate church, this one, particular hymn sheet should be in place. Or, rather, it was not baffling at all. The page had not yellowed, and had been torn from some book of holy song recently. Eli folded the paper, and put it into his inside pocket.

His head then flicked sideways. Though he saw nobody, Eli trained his weapon on the empty window. That prickle of warning was now a tattoo of burning needles.

Has he seen me? Morris wondered. Who cares? Morris drew his own Colt and fired through the church window. The rancher did not think that he would hit Eli, but he was not trying to. Luring Eli to this old building was but one of his chess moves. No, Morris was not going to kill Eli. There was too much fun to be had with him.

Eli ducked down behind the pulpit as the echo of the gunshot reverberated around the church. He was gasping, but too charged with anger to be afraid. Eli knew that there was only one way to win a game of cat and mouse: don't be the mouse.

Keeping his back to the wall, moving sideways like a crab, Eli slid over to the window. He turned to face outwards. Eli would barely have a single second to fire. In that instant, he sighted the shadowy figure peeping around the corner of the next building. Eli squeezed his trigger. As splinters of wood were repelled from the structure, Eli saw his assailant retreat.

Unwilling to surrender, Eli dived through the church window. Landing prone, Eli could hear the drum of escaping hoofs. He stood and ran after the sound, but his attacker had already vanished.

You will not get far, Eli vowed.

CHAPTER 10

At dawn on Wednesday, Bob again watched the sun ascend. It had barely been two days since the Strongs took them under their vulture wings. To Bob, though, Morriston felt like it was a thousand miles and a thousand years away. He and Adam had barely slept, and were exhausted. Yesterday's fighting and shooting drills had further drained them. Last night's so-called treat – half-cooked, unskinned rabbit – had sickened Bob. He had felt like a savage as he chewed the bloody, raw meat. The beast's hair had stuck to his lips and he had nearly broken his tooth on a bullet. The Connors were sustained only by their will to survive.

This morning, though, Charlie had an announcement of sorts over breakfast.

'We've got a little job to do today, boys. Me and Dwight are gonna need your help. We're riding on into Wells, a little town not far from here. There's a bank in that town, and we are going to hit it.'

This revelation was met by only hushed disbelief from the Connors. Though Adam and Bob were captives, Charlie withdrew two rifles from his saddle bags and handed one each to the Connors.

'You're going to need to be packing heat, boys,' he declared with total seriousness.

Charlie inspected the Connors' rifles, and Bob found this fastidiousness chilling. Charlie was making certain that the weapons were loaded. Bob was finding it difficult to contemplate the outrage which he was apparently going to commit.

'Now then, boys,' Charlie paused to take a noisy slurp of coffee, 'we will stick to our usual plan. The four of us will enter the bank. I will walk up to the clerk and give him a sack to fill with cash. Dwight will watch my butt. This time, Dwight, we have reinforcements. Adam and Bob will be our lookouts. They will watch the bank entrance. Anything happens, you call to us. You pull the trigger if you feel you need to.' Another theatrical sip. 'Then we ride like lightning. We will hitch our horses outside the bank, and mount up and ride soon as I say we're done.' Charlie rose to his feet: a general inspiring his troops. 'Are we ready, boys?'

Dwight replied with an energetic cheer. The Connors were in silent supplication.

'How about you, Bob?' Charlie asked. 'You ready?'

'Yes, sir.' Bob nodded meekly and compliantly. Though Bob could not even fake enthusiasm, Charlie favoured him.

There's no lying in the boy, Charlie thought. I see good things ahead from young Bob.

They set off. Adam seethed in his saddle. He was no coward, but was frustrated that his own dread of the Strongs was preventing his retaliation. Again, the Connors rode side by side with the Strongs flanking them. Both Adam and Bob were thinking the same thing. Each had an armed carbine strapped to his back. They did not quite understand why the Strongs were trusting them so, but Charlie and Dwight were hardly cautious types. With some rapid and well-aimed shots from the rifles, they could be rid of their captors. Reckless though the Strongs were, they were also deadly and unpredictable. The Connors did not resist, but rode on with them into Wells.

Drawing into the small town, Bob felt that he might explode. He had scarcely believed Charlie's announcement, but he was now seeing that his intentions were both true and toxic. The carbine on his back was comparatively lightweight, yet the weight of his imminent crime was pressing on his shoulders and his conscience.

As they rode their steeds the short distance to the bank, Bob felt that everybody was looking at him. The suffocating heat made Bob feel as if he was wearing a pantomime costume. It was not at all unusual for armed men to ride down the high street – not in this part of Wyoming. Nobody accosted them, but Bob felt as if he were walking into a trap.

Hitching their rides, it struck Bob that this was a grubby and pathetic exercise. The bank building was a small, brick construction. This was where farmers and saloon men deposited their takings. It was hardly a fortress protecting a treasure chest.

As they entered, there were a handful of customers in the poky foyer. There was but one desk with one teller. He was a greying man with spectacles, wearing a neat uniform. The clerk looked like an earnest sort. Bob felt truly regretful for the havoc he was about to cause him.

Charlie fired a shot into the air. Alarmed, the customers and clerk all faced him, rapt with fear. Dwight trained his Colt on the customers, and Charlie walked up to the teller's window. He stuffed a sack under the iron grille.

'Fill this bag with cash. Do it now,' Charlie commanded. 'We're the Strong brothers,' he added boastfully.

While he was guarding the bank door, Bob peeked over his shoulder at the Strongs. His heart hammered so powerfully that he could hear its blows in his ears. Bob was not afraid, though. Rather, he was a sac filled with venom. He was furious at how the Strongs terrorised innocents for a few bucks, and angry with himself for participating in the atrocity.

The teller reached into the drawer under his desk. He did not produce money, though, but a loaded revolver. Braver than he thought, the clerk's hands were rattling nervously as he raised the gun to Charlie.

The Strongs had grown very arrogant during their career of crime. They complacently assumed that a retiring bank clerk would meekly comply. Charlie never expected the teller to courageously resist. He had a coyote's sense of danger, though, and could see that something was up when the clerk reached into his drawer.

Predators such as the Strongs did not utilise reason nor persuasion. Charlie's reaction to the teller's daring ploy was as practised as a military drill. He pulled his own trigger, shooting the clerk dead.

Even Dwight stopped laughing.

CHAPTER 11

Though they were supposed to be lookouts, Adam and Bob turned back to look at the chaos. Their mouths were agape. Charlie had lost control of the situation. The Connors could sense his impotent fear. Bob had earlier divined that this raid would be unplanned and improvised, yet Charlie had been so cocksure.

Angry, Bob scowled at Charlie, who was not so vainly masterful now. Indeed, so panicked was Charlie that his face had reddened in frustration. He feebly growled unheeded instructions at the customers, who were all screaming, cursing or sobbing. Bob found that Dwight looked particularly pathetic. He flapped like a rag doll in a violent wind, desperately looking to his brother for direction.

Adam, too, looked like he was battling to restrain tears. His eyes darted back and forth between Bob and the Strongs: a rabbit who did not know which way to run.

Bob was certain of one truth: if the Strong gang did not act immediately, they would perish. The siren of the gunshots, and the wail of the bank patrons would attract lawmen.

Bob recalled an occasion when he and Adam had been left in charge of the store. Adam had served a customer who was a cantankerous old man. He had served the patron with his characteristic beaming enthusiasm, but in his zeal, had erroneously short-changed the customer. This had inflamed the shopper. Bob was no saloon doorman nor sheriff's deputy. However, as the sensible older brother, he had been compelled to referee. Inhaling deeply for courage, Bob had inserted himself between the two. Counting the cash calmly, Bob had righted the situation. The customer had walked away pacified, if not quite delighted with the service.

This was, oddly, how Bob felt when he took command of the robbery. He was the only man with dominion of his wits. There would be more bloodshed if the operation was left to the rabble around him.

Bob felt shameful when he shooed the customers away from Charlie with the butt of his rifle.

'Get back y'all! Listen to me! Get back against the wall!'

While Bob was inwardly terrified, his wild expression did not invite debate. The bank patrons complied. He next turned to Charlie, nudging him in the arm forcefully with his rifle butt.

'Get out of here, Charlie! Get! Get!'

Charlie appeared emasculated for a second, but Bob swore he saw a flicker of amusement in his eyes as Charlie obeyed. Bob's direction had calmed the Strongs, and Dwight was once again giggling shrilly as the four bank robbers bolted.

They mounted with a desperate speed, each of them

spurring their rides with cruel insistence. Bob heard a gunshot in the periphery, but did not spin around to see who it was. He knew it was the law. So intense was Bob's determined concentration that he was deaf to his pulse pummelling in his ears. He did not know where he was headed: Bob aimed his steed at the road out to the grass-lands and rode on.

The following few miles were a surreal dream. Bob remembered torturous nights when he was sickly as a child. The colours and shapes in his boyhood bedroom had been magnified and misshapen. Bob had not been certain whether he had been awake or asleep. Escaping from Wells, the grasslands and the ardent sun had the same queasy intensity.

Nobody spoke, and the only sound that Bob could detect was the constant tattoo of hoofbeats.

When, at last, Bob sensed his horse weakening, he halted the fugitive party. The lawmen of Wells had, thank-fully, been slow to reach their own mounts, and the Strong gang had once again absconded.

Breathless, the four riders rested for a few moments. They wheezed painfully for several minutes. When the Strongs began laughing, Bob saw that this ordeal was not yet ready to relent.

Bob did not share the others' mirth. He fixed Charlie with fury and outrage. So incensed was Bob that he could not sustain his silence.

'You think that's funny? You killed a man back there! How'd you think you'd get away with that?'

So smug was the look of pleasure on Charlie's fat face that he resembled an alligator.

'I do think that's funny, young Bob. It was a sticky

situation, but we made it out of there alive. Unlike the dumb bank teller!' Dwight shrieked his murderous approval of Charlie's little joke.

'You don't know what the heck you're doing, Charlie! If I wasn't there . . . I. . . .' The raw emotion was audible in Bob's voice. Inwardly, he was a whirlpool of conflicting sentiments. Charlie and Dwight had lost control of the robbery. It had been Bob who had taken charge. Bob's reserve under pressure meant that the four had escaped the bank alive. Yet, it was wrong to be proud. Bob had been an accomplice in a senseless killing. The Strongs' stupid gamble had not even led to any plunder.

Charlie could sense Bob's inner moral maelstrom. This was a weakness he could exploit.

'Take it easy, Bob. Now that teller pulled a gun on me. What else could I do? It was him or me. And you're right – what the heck would I have done without you? You were quick-thinking. Controlled. Calm. I need a man like you on my team.'

Bob was gripping his saddle horn so tenaciously he thought that his flushed fingers might snap. Charlie's empty flattery had irked him even more.

'You killed a man, Charlie,' Bob spat. The Strongs brayed in concert.

'Not for the first time,' he guffawed evilly. 'Now, we can't stick around too long. They'll never find us on the plains, but I know somewhere where we can rest and play for a time. Heck, you sure deserve a reward, Bob. I got some cash in my saddle bag, so let's go.'

Charlie spurred his steed with a blunt kick, and led the way. Adam had been shaken by the blundered robbery, but he would learn. Bob was pure potential. Charlie was very pleased with the progress which the Connors were making.

Charlie's boss would be pleased, too.

CHAPTER 12

Eli rode out from Beulah. He was heading back to the Morriston area, hoping to pick up the trail of his sons' abductors.

Focused as Eli was, it was a lonesome and monotonous ride across the plains. His drive to rescue his sons was undiminished, yet at times his thoughts meandered. The grasslands were a sea of brilliant green, repetitively sending wave after wave of gentle hills. As Eli's mind wandered, he recalled an encounter he had had as a young bounty hunter.

He had followed the trail to Cheyenne. In a major city, it was just as easy to blend into the impersonal throng as vanish below the prairie's stark horizon. In the café one evening, Eli made small-talk with a businessman from the East. Eli had asked the moneyman to elaborate on how he made his living. He had been a banker or commodities trader or some such thing. The businessman had been kind enough to explain. He was a young fellow straight out of college. Behind his spectacles were the intelligent and watchful eyes of an eagle.

The financier had produced a newspaper, and shown a

few articles to Eli.

'Partner – if the stock's about to go up, I buy. If it's about to go down, I sell.'

This much Eli understood, but he was still curious. He prodded the moneyman for more details.

'But how do you know which way the stock is going to move?'

The businessman paused and inhaled thoughtfully before responding.

'I studied mathematics in college. They taught me various models for predicting which way the markets will move – and they tend to be accurate. Perhaps to an outsider, it's just a haze of figures and facts. But me – I know what to look for. I can pick out key facts from all the data, and make a decision. After a time, I developed a feel for the patterns.'

The financier had been in Cheyenne to broker a deal between two corporations. Eli was hunting the leader of a gang of cattle thieves. The next day, Eli had found the thief in a whiskey trough, and the robber had drunkenly drawn on his hunter. Eli was too fast, though, and had shot his quarry dead.

Returning to the café that evening, Eli had again met the businessman.

'How did your finance deal go, partner?'

The financier was a little jolly, perhaps after a glass or two of champagne.

'Tremendous. I made a killing.'

'Me too,' Eli added.

Those days in Cheyenne were memorable to Eli because of the similarities he found between himself and the moneyman. Whereas their backgrounds had varied significantly, they were both talented and ambitious young men.

Nor would Eli ever forget the businessman's description of the patterns he could divine that were invisible to most. It reminded him of his own abilities as a tracker. Certain details were unmistakeable signs of a felon's illicit passage: broken blades of grass, hoofprints, disturbed rocks. These clues, while valuable, were always sparse and difficult to locate. As a hunter of beastly creatures, both animal and human, Eli had learned how to connect the jigsaw pieces.

On the plains, Eli found the remains of a makeshift camp. By the size of the ashes from the fires, and morsels of rotten, discarded, food, Eli deduced that there were four travellers. He did not doubt that this was the trail of his sons and their kidnappers.

They were drifting Eastwards. The design with which they left the marks from their camps signalled that they were possibly cleverly resting in random sites to throw their pursuers. Alternatively, they did not really know how to navigate. Eli suspected the latter. Whichever, there was only one significant settlement in this region: Wells.

Eli's mind did not rest for long in its reminiscences. His worries for his sons were so potent they were physically painful. Alone on the plains, with nobody to conceal his inner torture from, Eli often found himself weeping openly. Eli could not fathom what character of relationship had flowered between the four.

Eli's body and mind were sapped as he arrived in Wells. Although inwardly, Eli's love for his sons blazed on, he knew that the intelligent decision would be to rest – at least for one night. It would also be useful to glean some human intelligence.

Eli went to question local men at the saloon. They were very wary of strangers, but a couple of whiskies loosened lips.

Not a few hours ago, Eli learned, there had been a bank robbery. From the sound of it, the raid had been handled clumsily and a bank clerk had been senselessly slaughtered. This news gripped Eli.

'Tell me more, partner,' Eli urged his new drinking companion.

'Four armed men. Two of them were older, two of them were real young, like. Teenaged. Sounded to me like this robbery was badly planned. The four of them stormed in, and told the teller to hand over the goods. Dang it! The teller reached under his desk and pulled out a gun of his own. He was always such a quiet fellow. Had more guts than we thought. But he wasn't fast enough for these varmints. They opened fire and blew him away.'

'What happened next?' Eli impressed upon the drinker.

'Their leader took charge. He may only be a young buck, but this boy's already running an outlaw gang. This boy shooed everyone away, and led the gang out of there.'

'This young boy – what did he look like?'

'Dark-haired, they say. Stocky. Maybe nineteen years old.' Eli was alarmed, but fought to prevent his shock showing in his face. The barfly's description was an uncanny match for Bob.

The drinker went on. 'Might be just a kid, but he sounds like a nasty piece of work to me.'

CHAPTER 13

Stunned by the barfly's opinion, Eli covered his gaping mouth with his hand. He had kept quiet about his relationship to Adam and Bob. Ordinarily a taciturn man, Eli was concerned that his flicker of emotion revealed too much.

'Partner – you OK?'

Eli typically avoided strong drink, but had bought himself – and his new drinking partner – a couple of beers. While the bar was bustling, there was a murmuring, subdued atmosphere.

Like Morriston, Wells was a rural community whose townsfolk were dominated by farmers and ranchers. Eli's new acquaintance was a farmhand named Jake. He was as burly as a bear, with a stomach which also suggested animal appetites. Despite his powerful frame, Jake seemed a little reluctant to chat. Eli persuaded Jake that he was no gunny, only a shopkeeper in town for supplies. This half-truth and a glass of beer put Jake at ease.

'Jake – I can hardly believe what I'm hearin'. This outlaw gang is led by some young boy?'

Warming to his new friend, Jake slurped his beer

noisily. He had been labouring in the fields all morning, when his boss had sent him into town to run a few errands. Jake thought he had time for a glass of ale. The heat had been fearsome, and his flesh was reddened and sweaty. A single beer would have refreshed him, but Jake could hardly refuse the traveller's generosity when he bought a couple more.

'Yes, partner. That's the way it was. He was just a kid – but all the witnesses say that he was running the show, all right. He sounds deadly.'

Jake needed to return to the fields. He had enjoyed the visitor's company and kindness. Jake shook Eli's hand, swallowing it up in his ursine fingers and palm, before heading off.

Eli abandoned his half-drunk beer and sat on the boardwalk outside. The weight of his mission was testing him, and he could feel its gravity almost like a physical yoke on his shoulders. Slumped at the side of the road, he stared into empty space with maddened intensity. He sat indifferent to the curious glances of passers-by, who may have regarded him as some kind of drunk. The sting of the sun was nearly sizzling, yet Eli was unmoved by the heat.

The abductors had bolted from Wells very suddenly. Eli was confident that he could find their tracks. Low beasts such as these kidnappers left trails as surely as slugs left streaks of ooze in their passage. He knew he could find them, but he did not understand the bond between his sons and their captors.

Whether Adam and Bob had been willing abettors, or had been forced, Eli believed that the abductors had been the criminal masters in the affair. The rumours from

Wells were shocking.

Perhaps, though, he had been wrong. Eli wondered if his sons had been planning something from the outset. Moreover, the descriptions of Bob were extraordinary. Compared with Adam, Bob was very much the dutiful son. Bob was polite, gentle and well-meaning. He had always been very mature for his age. Yet the rumours likened him to a ringleader, a ruthless taskmaster.

They had been missing for days. What had his boys become in that short time?

So absorbed was Eli in his internal torture that he did not react to the grey shadow cast over him.

'You know what the punishment for public drunkenness is, sir?'

Though the figure was blackened against the relentless sun, Eli knew he was being addressed by a lawman. Mindful of the legal implications of his rogue pursuit, Eli cooperated. He was about to rise, when the sheriff put out a hand to help him to his feet.

'Eli Connor. I thought it was you. It's been years.'

Aided by the lawman's pincer grip, Eli stood and could see the sheriff clearly. It had been nearly twenty years, yet Eli remembered Sheriff Ryan Walters.

Eli nodded courteously in acknowledgement. He could tell by Walters's stern demeanour that it was no time for nostalgia.

'Follow me to my office, Eli.'

In his middle years, Walters's waistline had inflated. Indeed, he seemed to be struggling to contain his belly within his sheriff's uniform. He still retained his sandy, blond moustache and piercing, blue eyes. From his bounty hunter days, Eli recalled Walters being a stickler for the rules. They had not seen eye to eye, and Walters had regarded Eli's hunts as rivalry to his authority. Despite their past, in other circumstances, it might have been joyful to share a beer with Walters. Not today, though.

In the sheriff's office, Walters ordered Eli to sit. He complied, as the lawman sat at his desk.

'I know why you're here, Eli. Adam and Bob Connor? I heard about the kidnap in Morriston. And you know what happened here.' Walters was a softly-spoken man, which only seemed to emphasise the anger behind his words. 'I guessed they were your boys. Then, when you showed up, it confirmed my suspicions. What happened?'

'I don't know, Sheriff. But I'm on their trail. I want my sons safe and well and far away from these animals.'

'Powerful words, Eli. But you're talking like your boys are somehow victims in all this. That is not what I've heard.'

Eli was about to argue, but Walters raised a palm to silence him.

'I've never cared for bounty hunters, gunslingers, mercenaries – whatever you call yourselves. I do remember your tenacity and grit. Something tells me you've still got it. Now, we don't have a lot of crime in Wells. A murder? A kidnap – if that's what it was? I would never have foreseen that. I don't have a lot of manpower in Wells, and I sure as heck don't want a posse of untrained men being slaughtered. So I'm not going to interfere, Eli, much as I don't like it.'

At least, thought Walters, that's what John Morris told me to tell you.

Walters leaned back, and asked Eli a question he

already knew the answer to.

'Where do you reckon they're headed?'

Eli, too, had already guessed. 'Desolation.'

CHAPTER 14

'We're headed to Desolation, boys.' Charlie's announcement had made Dwight's demonic eyes glimmer with
excitement. 'We had a close shave back in Wells. I think
we could do with some partying.'

Desolation, Bob gathered from the snippets which
Charlie shared, was a tiny settlement in the hills. It was
not so much a township as a loose association of saloons,
gambling dens, and no sheriff. Desolation was hidden
away in the mountains, and was conceived as a resting
place for criminals on the run.

Charlie had shared a few stories of Desolation's
whiskey houses and wicked women.

Drawing closer, the rocky hills loomed in the distance.
Bob could not see them at first, but as they rode closer
and closer he began to discern the mountain's cruel
edges and ugly cracks. In contrast to the almost endless
green sea of the grasslands, the hills were a black and
repellent island. The mountains horrified the Connors: as
they drew nearer still, the brothers could not fathom how
they would navigate this grey, angular maze.

They had been riding north to reach Desolation, and

the temperature had dropped as sharply as the Connors' spirits. As the riders took their first steps into the rocky labyrinth, Bob wondered whether it was the air that chilled him, or his fear. The Connors followed the Strongs with apprehension. Charlie and Dwight seemed energised and excited. Unlike their aimless wandering on the prairie, the Strongs seemed to know the path to Desolation by memory.

'There it is, Dwight! There's Desolation!' Charlie exclaimed with great delight. 'Thar she blows!'

As the skies darkened and the cold worsened, Bob felt as if he were being bricked into a cave. The party was following a loose, pebble trail, though only the Strongs could make it out. Further down the path, the trail meandered around the curves of the hills, Charlie pointed out a pinprick of light. As they rode closer, Bob noticed other specks of illumination winking through the darkness like the devil. The Strongs were plainly very excited about their arrival in Desolation. Bob, though, took their high passions to be an omen of peril.

Desolation was eerily silent when they rode in. The quiet was torn by Charlie's eager whoops and Dwight's piercing shrieks.

They hitched their mounts on the rail outside what Bob guessed was a saloon. Charlie led them inside. The bar's interior was far more inviting than the bleak streets outside suggested. Warmed by a log fire, a number of customers chatted, drank, or played cards. As comfortable as the saloon was in the physical sense, the Connors were not at ease. They noticed the guests sneaking analytical glances at the new arrivals, trying to divine whether they were a threat, or marks to be exploited.

The atmosphere in the saloon was throbbing, if threatening. Bob sensed probing eyes flickering as the latest customers arrived. While the stares made Bob shiver, the Strongs were unperturbed. The cigar smoke mixed with the aroma of spilled whiskey could not mask a sickly, corrupt scent beneath. Bob saw that the clientele was exclusively male. There were a couple of women sitting on the laps of customers, and a female bartender.

These women were working, though. Bob could see why they were called painted ladies. The otherwise attractive young women had cheapened themselves with garish lipstick and cicada skins of mascara.

The Strongs led them up to the bar.

'What'll it be, boys?' The bartender was flirtatious, but did not seem to be performing the same role as the other women. She was a flame-haired, older woman. The barkeeper boasted an hour-glass figure which was uncomfortably contorted by the strains of her corset. Her air of confidence showed that she was the mistress of this establishment. She was polite and affable, but was plainly not a woman to be trifled with.

'Four whiskies, Suzanne.' Obviously, Charlie and the barmaid were acquainted. 'And send over a couple of girls to our table.'

'You got it,' Suzanne chirped with a wink. Her enthusiasm was contrived, though. She had poured drinks and arranged dirty dalliances for Charlie and Dwight many times. However, they had never brought guests before. These two handsome young men were different, though. Suzanne could sense it. There was something innocent about them.

The Strongs guided the Connors to a table, carrying

their whiskies. They slugged theirs, and ordered two more. The Connors' liquor sat before them untouched.

'Drink up, boys,' Charlie implored, licking his lips. Bob dutifully swallowed his as if it were bitter medicine. Adam raised his whiskey to his lips in a slower, defiant motion, tipping his glass with deliberate hesitation. As the liquor burned his maw, he eyeballed the Strongs. Adam's distaste for them was worse than his aversion to the cheap whiskey in his throat.

Charlie met Adam's insolent stare. 'I don't like that look, Adam. Don't worry – I know something that'll cheer you up.' As he spoke, they were joined at the table by Candy and Jezebel. The ladies did not hide their disgust very well when Charlie put his arm around each of them.

'Girls, I'd like to give my new recruits a little reward. How's about you take my young pals upstairs for a time?'

'Sure thing, honey,' squeaked Candy, relieved to be getting away from Charlie's unwelcome paws. The scarlet ladies took Adam and Bob by their hands.

'Don't be shy, boys,' Candy added kindly. Adam and Bob did not budge. It was not bashfulness: rather, a defiant resentment.

'Go on now, boys,' Charlie insisted. He flipped his jacket back to flash his Colt. The signal was not lost on the Connors, who rose to follow the women upstairs.

When Candy and Jezebel had finished, and the Connors returned downstairs, Suzanne sensed their air of dirty shame. They were not quite so innocent any more.

CHAPTER 15

The Connors sat back down in resignation. They felt soiled and ashamed. Worse than their regret, they wanted to take cold baths and scrub themselves pure again. Remorseful as he was, Adam was also perplexed. He did not understand why the Strongs had abducted them, and could not fathom the reasoning behind their illicit gifts of Candy and Jezebel. Adam could only surmise that the Strongs were cruelly playing mind games.

Bob was more pensive about the upstairs encounter. He did not know any better than Adam his captors' rationale. Bob suspected, though, that there was a callous logic to the Strongs' schemes.

'Enjoy yourselves, boys?' sneered Dwight. His skeletal grin was a smile of pure contempt. Disdainful though Dwight was, Bob could see that he was but an obliging pawn. Dwight deferred only to Charlie, and he probably did not know any better than Bob what was really going on.

The Strongs had ordered a fresh round of drinks during the Connors' shameful happenstances upstairs. Bob sipped at his whiskey. He was not accustomed to alcohol, and its intoxicating effects – plus his growing sense of dreadful resignation – emboldened him.

Bob addressed Charlie. 'So, what's this all about? Shooting lessons. Bank robbery. Those . . . women. Where are you taking us?'

Charlie knew that Bob was intelligent. He could see why he was curious. Nevertheless, Charlie had received quite precise instructions. Part of his orders required keeping the Connors in ignorant darkness.

'Never you mind, Bob. I'll look after you.' Charlie was keen to change the subject. 'Heck, I've shown you a real nice time tonight, ain't I?'

Bob was not reassured, and petulantly slugged the rest of his whiskey. He could sense that Charlie was resisting his probing. Bob already felt wretched. His experiences under the Strongs, and particularly his bedroom session, had clawed his soul downwards. Bob did not believe he retained much more spirit. He almost wanted the Strongs to finally crush him underfoot.

Bob rose and moved around the table to Charlie. The insolent regard with which he fixed Charlie unnerved Adam. Adam had an inkling that there would be an imminent, and ugly, confrontation.

Charlie could sense it, too. He had won or lost literally hundreds of fistfights during his years. The invisible and furious energy radiated by Bob warned him. Bob was about to crouch to meet Charlie at eye level, but Charlie was rattlesnake rapid. He sprang to his feet, and backhanded Bob with venom. This swiftly efficient blow startled Bob. The strike sent him staggering. Adam rushed to steady his brother with an arm over his shoulders. He led Bob back to his seat, Bob glowering poisonously.

Though Dwight tittered shrilly, and the saloon's customers rested their chatter to gawk, Charlie experienced a pang of guilt. Though he had delivered countless pummellings and worse, he felt a touch of regret. Striking Bob was, Charlie imagined, like chastising a son.

'Now you watch your step, Bob,' Charlie commanded. 'I need a man like you. Don't give me cause to hurt you.' He noted that Bob was so incensed that he seemed to glow.

Charlie reached into his jacket where he kept his secondary Colt in its holster. He could see the Connors squirm as he withdrew it, so smiled to reassure them. Charlie rested the gun flat on the table and slid it over to Bob. It made a gentle yet menacing, grinding sound on the coarse wood.

'Take this, Bob. I trust you. You're too smart to try something on me. Even if you did, Dwight and I'd . . . well, you won't try nothing.'

Noticing that the weapon was loaded, Bob stuck the Colt in his belt. Bob did not wear a holster, and the gun hung loosely and uncomfortably from his waist. It amused Charlie to see the weapon suspended so clumsily.

For one night, Charlie had endured enough babysitting. Desolation was where crooks on the run came to party. It was time to start enjoying the evening. Charlie drew a wedge of dollar bills from his pocket. His patron was paying him well for childminding. He slid these over to Bob, as well.

'Fetch us a round of drinks, Bob. Let your hair down, dang it.'

Bob took the bills and approached the bar. His Colt wedged awkwardly in his belt, he was naively advertising his inexperience with the weapon. Bob did not care to dwell on Charlie's reasoning for entrusting him with a gun: arming him to disarm him. He was tiring of Charlie's psychological games, and unwilling to play.

'Four whiskies, please, Suzanne.' Charmed, Suzanne obliged. Despite the company he kept, and his disgraceful tryst upstairs, this young man had not forgotten his manners.

As Suzanne poured the drinks, a grossly fat drinker in a Stetson waddled up to Bob. He was a drunk bully and, seeing Bob's youth and evident naïvete, thought he would enjoy some spiteful sport. Perhaps he could even hustle a few bucks.

'Boy – you old enough to drink?' the boozer chortled, spraying Bob with spittle. Still enraged by Charlie's backhand, Bob struggled to remain calm.

'Please, partner. Just buying a few drinks.'

'Where are you from, boy?' the drunk insisted.

'Excuse me, suh.'

The whiskey hog shoved Bob, smugly grinning at his own imagined audacity. 'Asked you a question, boy.'

Perhaps the Strongs had trained him too well, for Bob instinctively snatched his Colt, cocked the weapon, and fired. The bullet made a sound like a camera flash as it hit the pillow of the saloon sloth's fleshy gut. He collapsed to his knees clutching his rent belly, his final facial expression one of incredulity.

There was an instant of silence before a chorus of whoops and cheers filled the saloon. The first ones to embrace Bob were the Strongs. As they hugged him close to their breasts, their pride practically shone. Bob attracted a throng of admirers, applauding and congratulating him.

Nobody noticed Suzanne's men dragging the glutton's bloodied remains away.

As Bob swallowed whiskey after whiskey pressed on him, he noticed Adam sitting alone at the table. Their eyes met, and for Adam, it was as if he was staring into an endless black well. Adam did not understand what his brother was becoming.

Bob recognised that glint of incomprehension, but it did not quell his cheer.

Darn, Bob thought. Killing feels good.

CHAPTER 16

The Strongs' attentions and backslapping did nothing to warm Bob to them. In slaying the overbearing drunk, Bob had acted not so much mindlessly as from an urge in his gut. Bob knew that he ought to feel appalled by himself, yet he was electrified. His assassination of the boozer had ignited a blaze of energy in him. Despite whiskey after whiskey, his murderous fire was unextinguished.

Nevertheless, though the Strongs embraced him as they would a long-lost kinsman, Bob could not forget his circumstances. Charlie and Dwight had scraped him and Adam away from their home at gunpoint. Bob could still not fathom why. While he did not regret killing the fat barfly, Bob was a different species to the Strongs. Wasn't he?

The death of the glutton (who, not thirty minutes after his destruction, was interred under a thin layer of gravel on a boot hill) had also charged the saloon. The bar's contented murmurs had been magnified into thrilled laughter and a buzz of screaming chatter. At home in Morriston, such an event as a shooting would have deadened the atmosphere of the whole town. In Desolation's whiskey trough, though, a death was only an amusement.

'Good work, son. Liked the way you offed that fat pig,' congratulated Charlie, for perhaps the twentieth time, as he put yet another whiskey in Bob's hand. Bob was leaning against the bar, and his unexpected glimmer of cocksureness was not lost on Charlie. 'When I put that Colt in your hand, I knew that something big was going to happen,' he added.

While Bob could not deny his own feeling of arrogant invulnerability, Charlie's comment irked him. Had he been manipulated? Had Charlie predicted what would happen?

'What do you mean?' snapped Bob. Now, he was not merely obstinate and defiant. Bob was fixing Charlie directly in the eye.

You're not afraid of me, are you? Charlie thought. Good stuff.

'I just had a good feeling about you, Bob. If you must know,' he nodded surreptitiously to Adam, still alone at the table, 'you're my favourite. A little voice in my head told me that you're different. Adam's got potential, sure, but you've got the brains and the balls to deal with a nasty situation.' Bob had somehow known what Charlie would say next. 'You're just like me, Bob. Just like me.'

Enraged, Bob spun away from Charlie to face the bar. He was not angry because Charlie's words were so offensive. Bob was furious because he feared that Charlie had reason. Was Bob transforming into a new creature? Or was Bob acting as the man he always was – but did not realize?

He felt for the Colt, which was again stuck uncomfortably into his belt. The weapon had now cooled and was icy against his fingertips. His head swung back to glower at Charlie. Charlie could sense what Bob was thinking about and smiled in approval. He was pleased to see Bob in psychic turmoil.

Further angered by Charlie's grin, Bob turned his attention back to the bar.

'Two more, Suzanne.' The barkeep nodded in acknowledgement, but did not speak. Bob Connor – if that was his name – had changed. He was no longer the courteous boy who had walked in not two hours ago. Suzanne dealt with the human equivalent of poison every night. Her customers were thieves, gangsters and killers. Yet it saddened her to see this young man sullied so. He looked barely nineteen. He had had a lifetime of possibilities ahead of him. Now, his conscience would forever be tainted by another man's blood.

Deliberately ignoring the Strongs, Bob carried the whiskies over to Adam's table. Perhaps it was his own dampened zeal, or possibly the clientele was now tiring of discussing the killing over and over, but the ambiance seemed subdued. Sitting back down with Adam hardly cheered Bob. His younger brother had typically been so boisterous and alive with energy. He now seemed withered and shrunken, and looked on Bob with timid eyes. To Adam, Bob appeared to be much like a stranger.

Sliding the whiskey glass over to Adam, Bob noted that Adam had not yet touched his last drink. They sat unspeaking for a little while before Bob broke their loaded silence.

'You OK, Adam?'

Adam took a moment before responding. He seemed to be composing himself for a difficult task. 'Why'd you kill that man?'

Bob had an inkling that this question was coming. In truth, Bob did know why, though it was impossible to articulate his thoughts and feelings. When he had squeezed the trigger on that fat bully, Bob had been acting on a purely animal level. Bob sipped a little whiskey before responding.

'It was pure gut instinct, Adam. That drunk dolt was pushing me around. Maybe all that shooting practise out on the plains rubbed off on me. I wasn't thinking about it when I shot the fat fool. And I don't mean I was being dumb. I mean my fingers had a life of their own.' Bob took another sip, for he had also predicted Adam's next question.

'What was it like?' This was not ghoulish fascination. Adam was trying to decipher who the stranger sitting next to him was. Bob paused before answering.

'It was like a drug, Adam. Better than liquor or opium. I felt invincible: ten feet tall.'

Adam did not comment, but his look of wary apprehension spoke for him. He had already been fearful of the Strongs, and now feared that he had a third enemy. Bob reached over and put a comforting hand on Adam's forearm. Adam was not reassured.

The saloon did not ring a bell for the last orders. Instead, Suzanne alerted her customers that the bar was closing by firing a shotgun through an opened window.

'Party's over, you bums! Get out of here!'

The Strongs drunkenly staggered over to collect their charges. Charlie was a little jolly when he commanded them.

'All right, boys. Time to bed down. Hope you enjoyed. Tomorrow, it's another long ride. There's somebody we'd like you to meet.'

CHAPTER 17

Eli had paid for a room for the night in Wells. As desperate as he was to find his sons, it was senseless to ride out onto the plains when the grasslands were masked by darkness. Before retiring, Eli had attempted to eat a good meal in the hotel's dining room. This notion was borne by Eli's knowledge that he should eat, rather than any great hunger.

In the hotel's restaurant, Eli had dreamily sawed and poked at his steak and potatoes. He was indifferent to the gentle clink of the other guests' cutlery. The pleasing aroma of gravy and roast meat from the kitchens only strengthened the appetites of the other diners, but Eli did not even notice. He was ordinarily wakeful and alert, but so engrossed was Eli in his painful reverie that the other patrons' odd looks and bemused muttering did not register with him.

Eli did not know how long he had been entranced at the table when he came around. The staff were dimming the lanterns, but were too wary of the peculiar stranger to eject him from the dining hall. Eli found his food cold and uneaten, but absent-mindedly cut into little pieces. He half-wondered how the plate had arrived there.

The hall was deserted now, and Eli felt a little like the last drunk in the saloon, impotently refusing to leave. He rose and ascended the wooden steps to his cheap room, the hotel ghostly quiet but for his padded footsteps. The silence only emphasised Eli's tortured lonesomeness. He shivered, not from the evening's plunging temperature, but from anxiety. Eli's longing for his sons was a physical pain.

Frustrated that his manhunt had to take pause for the night, Eli slammed his bedroom door behind him. He did not care if he disturbed the other guests. Even if he had, none of them would have dared come to accost that stranger with the crazed countenance about him.

Eli lit the oil lamp and sat on his spartan bed. Wells did not receive many travellers, and the plain hotel room befitted the town's veneer of welcome. The dim, orange glow of the lamp mirrored Eli's drowning spirits. Yet the dancing flame within the lantern's glass prison also mimicked Eli's burning love. Though he was physically and emotionally drained, Eli's scorching dedication to his pursuit smouldered undiminished.

He was in turmoil, though. His feelings meandered from anger to sadness to listless indifference. Sat on the bed, and ignoring the itch from his new bed-mates, Eli was once again mesmerised. A memory he had not recalled for many years returned.

Adam and Bob had been perhaps nine and ten. They

were still in school, and spent their Saturdays working in the store. His sons were well-behaved boys. Adam could be a little cheeky, but he was never in trouble. Bob was particularly mature for his age. When Eli and Cassie received an invitation to dinner at their neighbours' house, they thought they could trust their boys to behave for one night when they went out.

Eli, rapt by his recollection, did not realize that he was smiling to himself. In Morriston, your nearest neighbour was a good two miles away. Eli and his wife thought nothing of the short journey. It had been a comfortably warm summer evening. Walking arm in arm, Eli and Cassie had chatted and giggled about nothing all the way. The sun had been retreating, but not even the stretching fingers of grey shadows could blur Cassie's magnetic beauty. Her golden locks and blue eyes sparkled despite the darkness. Not for the first time, Eli thanked the heavens for his great fortune.

Dinner with the neighbours had also been joyful. Eli had become a new man since sharing his life with Cassie. Years earlier, Eli's mind had been consumed by nothing but his next arrest. That night, over bowl after bowl of beef stew, Eli had gossiped and shared atrocious jokes that nonetheless caused roars of laughter.

The Connors shared heartfelt embraces with their friends before their stroll home. Eli was armed, of course, but Morriston (at least then) tended to be a peaceful town. The couple were not bothered by brigands nor outlaws, but on arriving home, their house looked like it had been burgled.

Central to the disarray, Eli had found Adam and Bob fighting. Or rather, Adam had been laying into his brother while Bob cowered behind hands covering his face.

Eli would not let two naughty boys ruin such an enjoyable evening, but he had to play the part of the strict father. He had barked instructions, and the boys had rapidly reversed the mess they had created.

His sons had each received a stroke from the slipper before bed. Interestingly, Adam – the more brash and boisterous son – had cried childish tears after his chastisement. Bob had steeled himself to the slipper's bite, and dutifully apologised before going to sleep.

Eli had witnessed this so many times with his sons. Bob was stocky and tall, but was kind and gentle. Bob was big enough to defeat Adam in a fight, but he always deliberately surrendered to Adam's fists. Eli suspected that Bob did not have the heart to beat up his little brother. This streak of goodliness in Bob gladdened Eli.

The blissful memories faded away, and Eli again found himself in the dingy hotel room. He undressed, and would try to enjoy some rest – even if it meant staring into the darkness for hours. The fears haunting Eli remained, but his happy recollection cheered him a little. His sons were in danger – but Eli was fortunate to have somebody worth fighting for.

The abduction was also half the mystery. Eli wanted to know the import of the string tie and the identity of his assailant in Beulah. There were many strands to this cobweb of deception, and Eli was determined to follow them, whatever monstrous spider waited at their centre.

He tried to draw some solace from his memory. Eli was certain that Bob would be watching over his younger brother. The stories from Wells had alarmed Eli, but they were only rumours. Bob had a touch of kindness and decency that would never be corrupted.

At least, that's what he hoped.

CHAPTER 18

Eli may have spent the whole night staring into the gloom, for he was awake to watch grains of dust dancing in the rays of the sun. He was pleased that the wretched night was over with and it was light enough to ride again. Turbulent as Eli's thoughts were, he prayed that the day would bring a sliver of hope, however thin.

After last night's pathetic failure to ingest a hearty meal, Eli did not even bother to attempt breakfast. He gulped cup after cup of bitter coffee in the dining room, only rising to leave the table when his belly was full.

Wells had received him cordially, if coldly, but he was glad to be leaving. Mounting and setting off, the sun had fully risen in the East. The heavens were a serene, faded blue and Eli inhaled the rich smell of the grasslands ahead. But for the troubles that lay ahead of him, it was a beautiful day.

Desolation was north of Wells. It would take the best part of a day to reach the mountain trail to the deadly township. Eli forced himself to concentrate on the ride ahead. His wrought imagination created dozens of different and perilous scenarios for his sons. Eli fought to close his mind to these frightening visions. As he rode harder and harder, those images of danger kept returning and returning. Eli had to wipe his unshaven face clean several times, but he was not certain whether he was brushing away perspiration or tears.

At last, the mountains appeared in the distance. At first, they resembled an ugly, black rock perched incongruously on the horizon. Drawing closer, Eli could discern the hills' broken, grey teeth and hideous, grasping claws. He trembled. Twenty years ago, Eli would have approached the mountain's angular claws fearlessly. Indeed, he had pursued his quarries to Desolation several times. The thought of his sons in the clutches of evil men hidden away in these hills was repellent. He steeled himself as he started up the mountain trail.

Though it had been decades, Eli's memory remained as cutting as a bayonet. The trail had not been designed by men. Rather, it was a jigsaw of rock platforms and pebbled slopes that were not too steep to ride on. Eli rode with great caution, subconsciously happy to be distracted from the nightmare pictures in his mind.

Desolation was an outlaw outpost. Eli wondered how the saloon there, so remote, could remain stocked with whiskey and beer. Hoodlums laying low would pay a pretty penny or an ugly dollar for booze, he supposed. When he sighted the settlement on the path ahead, Eli drew breath. While he was no lawman, the rodents who inhabited Desolation would be able to sense that Eli was not one of them. They would view him as either prey to be exploited, or a hunter to be shunned. Moreover, while criminals did not tend to live very long nor boast great intellects, they had long memories. Eli wondered if any of the township's denizens would know or remember him.

Eli drew into Desolation in the early afternoon. There were only a few individuals around. Most of the town were likely sleeping off their hangovers. Gently trotting horseback along the stony high street, Eli's nape prickled. It was as if he was riding through a forest riddled with coyotes hidden in the bushes. Dozens of unseen eyes were studying this stranger, guessing whether he would be an opportunity or a threat.

Eli dismounted and hitched his ride to the rails outside the saloon. The bar would be a good place to start: bartenders heard everything. Entering the saloon, he found only a handful of customers. Their eyes darted to measure up the stranger who had walked through the batwings. There was little chatter as Eli approached the bar.

'What can I get you, stranger?' Suzanne was long accustomed to the ways of violent and deceitful men. This visitor to her bar was different, though. There was something about the man's comportment that suggested strength and dedication. She had also noticed him surreptitiously scanning her saloon like a hovering hawk. This was not a man to be trifled with.

'Just a beer, barkeep.' Eli would have preferred to keep a clear head, but supping lemonade or merely water in such an establishment was laughably naïve.

Eli did not want any undue attention. As Suzanne served his drink, though, the prickle on his nape burned like a candle.

Eli turned to see a drinker approaching him. Had Eli's innate sense of danger not alerted him, the man's reek would have given him warning enough. The young man was not greatly older than his sons. He was unshaven and unwashed, with few teeth and fewer scruples. The crook thought that he would test Eli's pluck. He chewed tobacco as noisily as he could, then spit it out contemptuously at Eli's feet.

'Give me your money.' He was not given to bashfulness nor bathing.

Eli did not respond. The varmint meant to reach for his six-gun. Eli noticed the slightest movement of the thief's hand, a gesture Eli had learned to recognise the hard way. Before the bar bum's hand had moved an inch, he found himself reeling backwards, blood coursing down his face, his nose shattered.

Haven't done that for a while, thought Eli. He turned back to his beer, extending and contracting his sore fingers. It pained him to grip the beer glass.

'You've cut yourself,' Suzanne commented. Eli noticed that the impact of his blow had split the skin on his knuckles. 'That's one heck of a right cross you got there, mister.' She admired him. This stern traveller had bested a man young enough to be his son, then calmly returned to his beer. Nobody in this darned snake-pit of a town was going to trouble him.

'I'm . . . out of practise,' Eli admitted, modestly.

'You remind me of somebody. Something similar happened last night. He didn't have any patience for saloon slobs, neither.'

'Go on,' Eli pressed.

CHAPTER 19

Suzanne could sense that Eli was unlike the pathetic lowlifes who made up her clientele. His would-be attacker had fled, leaving a spotty trail of blood that Suzanne would have to mop up. There were still a few customers in the main bar. Though they outwardly sipped their beers with indifference, Suzanne knew they were straining to eavesdrop. This was the curse of being a criminal: perpetual guardedness. They were desperate to know what Suzanne and Eli were discussing, hoping perhaps to extract some valuable information.

Suzanne took Eli's cut hand in hers, inspecting the red slits on his fingers. As she did, their eyes met. Suzanne knew that they could both feel it: the connection of their digits conducted an invisible current of electricity through their bodies. The two remained silent for a moment.

'Follow me, stranger. I've got some clean water in my backroom. I'll give those knuckles a scrub.' She led Eli by the hand into the chamber behind the main saloon. Suzanne did not care what the drinkers in the bar would report to their brigand brethren, nor what embellishments they might add. Indeed, in her time she had done foul things with fouler men. Suzanne was rather glad that the gossip would link her to this dashing mystery man.

Eli, too, was grateful for Suzanne's attentions. He thought for a second that being taken by the hand by a woman would signify weakness. Eli quickly brushed the thought away. Indeed, he admitted to himself that it would be wise to cleanse the cuts on his knuckles.

In the backroom, Suzanne filled a bowl with clean water, and lathered up the water with carbolic soap. The silence was charged with their shared attraction. Suzanne was alluring in a very different way to Cassie. Whereas his late wife was an angel to Eli and his sons, Suzanne had a touch of devilishness about her, a quality only emphasised by her flaming hair. She was no saint, Eli mused, but Suzanne's warmth and kindness were palpable.

Eli caught himself. He had been a widower too long, but concentrated on his pursuit.

'Suzanne,' Eli entreated. 'Please tell me about this incident last night.'

Eli's good manners confirmed Suzanne's inkling. His courtesy reminded her of Bob's politeness. Eli's handling of his assailant mirrored the way Bob neutralised that fat bully.

'Four men rode in last night. I knew two of them: the Strong brothers. They show up in Desolation from time to time. The two others were young men: perhaps eighteen or nineteen. I think their names were Adam and Bob Connor.' Suzanne felt a frisson run through Eli's fingers. 'Now, Adam and Bob were respectable boys. They looked out of place with the Strongs. The four of them drank a few whiskies, when Bob came up to the bar. This fat fellow – I think his name was Gordo – started shoving Bob around.'

Suzanne paused. She took Eli's hand from the bowl and dried it with a towel. 'Now this is a rough town, but I did not expect what happened next. This polite young gentleman drew his gun and shot Gordo dead.'

Eli was speechless, and Suzanne continued.

'Now Gordo was a nasty piece of work. Shooting, thieving. He also had a . . . fondness for handsome young men. Nobody's going to miss Gordo. In fact, it was party time afterwards.'

Were he not so stupefied and shocked, Eli might have wept. What had these Strong brothers done to his sons? From the rumours, Bob had been transformed for the worse.

'Come on now, Eli,' Suzanne cajoled flirtatiously. 'What's your connection? You ain't no travelling salesman.'

Eli felt that he could trust Suzanne.

'Adam and Bob Connor are my . . . sons. They were abducted on Monday night. The lawmen back home in Morriston won't do nothin', so I have to find them. I've heard that they've been involved in a robbery in Wells. And now this!'

Enraged, Eli pulled away from Suzanne, turning away from her. She was not surprised that Bob was his son: both possessed the same blend of courteousness and callousness. Suzanne did not volunteer details of Adam and Bob's trysts with Candy and Jezebel. Eli was emotional enough already.

Suzanne gently rubbed Eli's shoulder. Despite himself,

Eli's skin again tingled. He turned back to face her.

'Suzanne – is there anythin' else you can tell me? Do you know where they are headed?'

'They camped up for the night and rode off at first light. The Strongs spoke of following a mountain trail North East. Back out to the plains.'

'I'll find it. Thank you, Suzanne.'

Eli was about to leave, when Suzanne lay her palm flat on Eli's breast.

'Be careful, Eli. You've got a pure heart. Your sons need you – but they need you in once piece.'

Eli nodded, but did not have time for Suzanne's reassurances, however heartfelt. He pushed past her. Seconds later, Suzanne heard the pounding of hoofs on the stony ground outside.

Suzanne sighed. She was not given to sentimentality nor indulgent daydreaming. While there was no denying the chemistry she shared with Eli, the man had much more important things on this mind. It had been a pleasure to share some time with him, however brief.

Suzanne returned to the bar. It was not a throng this afternoon, and the bustle or otherwise of the saloon could not be predicted. The species of men that passed through Desolation did not keep to a timetable.

She took the mop from behind the bar and walked over to the bloodstains which Eli had drawn from his attacker. Moving across the bar floor, one of her patrons could not resist comment.

'What you get up to with that stranger, Suzanne? Anything ... salacious?' he hissed. He had a filthy, greying beard and a gap in his teeth that made him lisp. The observer was a little older than Suzanne, but not too old for a kick in the groin.

Flailing painfully from her ruthless delivery, the commentator did not question Suzanne further.

CHAPTER 20

Suzanne's violent repulsion of the customer gladdened her. She smirked proudly as the strokes of her mop wiped away the spots of blood from the wooden floor. Her victim's pained groans had faded now, and he had limped away. Hopefully, Suzanne thought, you're a little wiser now.

The afternoon returned to its quiet. Later, the saloon would likely be as riotous as usual. To busy herself, Suzanne pressed on with her cleansing of the floor. Fresh blood, as Suzanne well knew, could be mopped up with ease. However, sprinkles of gunpowder, spilled whiskey and beer, cigar stubs and other substances which Suzanne did not care to dwell on, had accumulated. Her saloon floor was a collage of cruelty. The mop would give it a glistening sheen for a few minutes. It would only be a sheen, though. Nothing would ever truly shift the filth.

Nor could the mop purify her memories. The scratches and stains on the wooden floorboards were scars from countless grisly encounters which her saloon had hosted. Suzanne preferred to do her own housework. It was her bar, at least in name. Though she had a small crew of barmen and scarlet women under her, Suzanne led by example. She paid her staff well enough, but they had plenty to endure already. Suffering insults from drunks, and throwing them out when enough was enough, would be difficult for a barkeeper in a peaceful town. In Desolation, bartending to killers and outlaws could be deadly.

Suzanne hoped that her mop strokes would also somehow wash away her thoughts of Eli. He was plainly a decent and dedicated man. No lovesick schoolgirl was she, and Suzanne was not fantasising about being rescued by Eli. Rather, she was concerned for the man and his sons. Eli, brave though he was, did not understand the peril he was riding into.

Inevitably, thoughts of Eli led to thoughts of her own past. Though she tried not to dwell, the images in her mind played on like an intoxicated raconteur stubbornly refusing to shut up. Suzanne gripped the mop handle furiously, making awkward, powerful thrusts. Yet her mop strokes impotently failed to arrest the torrent of unwelcome memories.

Suzanne had never known her father, nor had she ever been interested in asking. Her earliest years had been spent in a house of ill-fame in Cheyenne. Suzanne's own mother had been a painted lady. The establishment provided a simple boarding-house behind the front rooms where guests were entertained. A number of courtesans had children.

Suzanne was guarded about who she revealed her individual history to. So many stomachs seemed to sicken when she shared her story. Suzanne accepted that the notion of a young girl raised in a brothel was visceral, yet her earliest recollections were joyful.

The demi-mondes, at the madam's insistence, operated behind a Chinese wall to their families. The children never strayed across this invisible line. Their business was a sleazy one, yet lucrative. All the fallen women paid for their children to attend school.

Outsiders always imagined that Suzanne's mother was some species of beast, selfishly exposing her child to dangerous baseness for the sake of a few dollars. In fact, though at first Suzanne did not understand her mom's nocturnal disappearances, she was loved and cherished. She felt that she had a dozen mothers, and a dozen brothers or sisters. To the astonishment of strangers, this secret sisterhood was happy and safe.

When the children of the harlots became adults, they often moved on to good jobs, marriage, or even college. Unfortunately, there were sometimes stragglers. The madam was loath to introduce them to the family business. Instead, she found odd jobs for these late bloomers around the establishment: barkeepers, receptionists or cleaners.

Suzanne was such a straggler. Smart though she was, Suzanne was also restless and irascible. At school, she had been a regular inhabitant of the naughty chair. Her red hair reflected the inferno in her soul. It was this fiery quality that led to Suzanne saving a life, and her own damnation.

Aged eighteen, Suzanne was a dogsbody in the house of ill-fame. She had been reluctantly performing an errand one evening when she was alerted by screaming from one of the private rooms. This was not the familiar report of feigned ecstasy: Suzanne's sister within was being assaulted.

The house retained security men to protect the sisters from customers who were base in violent ways. Suzanne lacked the patience to summon them as she kicked the door open. She saw the customer, an elderly man not yet so frail that he could not subdue a young woman, with his hands around the courtesan's throat. Her sister's face was reddened by welts. That relentless fire in Suzanne's belly exploded.

She noted a weapon in a holster on the Welsh dresser. Under house rules, guns were forbidden, but this fiend had slipped one through.

Many years later, Suzanne had yet to decipher the violent haze that followed. She remembered looking down on the dead man. The Colt had still been warm in her hand. Her ears had been ringing from the gun's blast. Suzanne had pulled the trigger on that sick-minded creep. Years and years later, she regretted nothing.

The dead customer had turned out to be wealthy and powerful. Suzanne may have gone to the noose, but for the fortuitous presence of a customer more powerful still.

An occasional guest of the establishment, John Morris had been in the adjacent room. Hearing the disturbance, he had taken pause from his dalliance, dressed, and found Suzanne, armed, standing over the dead old goat. The bloodied scene did not trouble Morris. He had seen and done worse things. Morris had an instinct for opportunity. He could use a woman like Suzanne in a saloon he owned, which was hidden away in the mountains.

These reminiscences made Suzanne's arms stiffen. Her

mopping had become laboured and tiresome. She was about to give up when she shivered. Suzanne had stepped into the shadow of a very tall, powerfully-built man.

She had never been one to defer to men. In her saloon she had faced innumerable individuals with less honour than rats. Yet she could never quite look Morris in the eye. He was not exactly her boss. Rather, Morris was an unseen force, manipulating her from afar.

Morris did not speak when Suzanne turned to face him. She well knew what she had had to do.

'I told him, Mr Morris,' she explained with uncustomary meekness. 'Eli is on his way through the mountain pass. He's well on his way to your ranch.'

CHAPTER 21

The mountain trail was a slippery passage of loose pebbles on slopes that rose and fell sharply. The Strongs were typically reckless horsemen, but even they had to slow their pace to climb the hazardous inclines.

'So where are you taking us now?' Bob had demanded. Since his masterful handling of the robbery, and his unexpected – yet brilliant – elimination of the fat drunk, Bob had become flippant and resentful. While this defiance made him more difficult to handle, Charlie liked this change in him. Despite his violent experiences and forced abduction, Bob was more than a little cheeky.

Indeed, Charlie saw this as a similarity with him. The Strongs' string of crimes had been more wild gambles than daring exploits. In spite of the bloodshed they had caused and suffered, the Strongs had always ridden away laughing.

'Told you, son. Somebody we'd like you to meet,' Charlie had answered enigmatically. Almost unconsciously, Charlie had taken to calling Bob son. Charlie did not mean to be condescending. It was a true term of endearment. Charlie had never fathered any children. He

101

had never even had a sweetheart. Charlie had nevertheless begun to fancy himself as a surrogate father to Bob.

The Strongs led the way through the mountain trail. Unknown to their charges, they were heading back out West to the plains. From Morriston to Wells to Desolation back to the grasslands was a somewhat circuitous route, but that was all part of the Strongs' instructions. Charlie glanced back at his wards. He was reassured to see Bob seething in his saddle, while Adam was so frightened he had paled.

Charlie's cuckoo fatherhood of the Connors reminded him of his own father. Strong Senior had been a drunkard, saloon brawler and petty thief. Yet Charlie's father had been courageous and faithful in his own manner.

The Strongs had never known their mother. For as long as they could remember, their father had marched them from town to town. Charlie and Dwight had never spent a single day in school, nor created any lasting friendships. Since they were infants, they had been each other's only companion.

Their father had been a drifter and a small-time crook. Even as children, the Strongs had been constantly on the run. Zeke Strong, their progenitor, had received many thrashings from people he had tried to rob, or had otherwise affronted. He had always been too cunning for the lawmen, though, and had disappeared before they ever raised their inquisitive ears.

Zeke had been content to pick pockets, shoplift, burgle, and on one occasion steal a cow. Charlie recalled the time when he and Dwight had assisted their father to lead away the hapless animal. This was an episode which demonstrated Zeke's reckless dearth of foresight, a care-lessness that his sons would inherit.

Zeke had stirred his sons from their beds late one night. The Strongs occasionally stayed in boarding houses when their father could afford it, but more often they slept under the stars, or in improvised tents. The night of the cattle robbery, Charlie and Dwight had been fast asleep under their blankets. Zeke had never told them he was planning to steal a cow. Indeed, their father had not exactly planned the theft. Rather, he had been chewing the idea over as he lay in bed, and impulsively decided to make a go of it.

A farmer kept a number of milk cows in a corral over the hill. Charlie remembered a chill in the air that night. The brothers had initially been disgruntled to be sum-moned from their slumber. However, when their father had explained his ploy, they had been thrilled. They were probably around nine or ten years old at the time. Dwight's questions had been incessant, and Zeke had to shush him.

The song of the crickets in the air, and the grass squelching underfoot, the Strong clan had made its way over the hill. Led by their father, they climbed over the stone wall. Zeke feared that the sounds would alert the cows' owner. Zeke knew that he had to act rapidly.

The cow he chose did not resist as he tied a rope around its neck. In fact, the animal mooed curiously, and seemed faintly amused as Zeke led her away. Zeke glanced around furtively, nervously dragging the cow away as his sons held the wooden gate open.

Returning down the hill, the Strongs were as excitable as if it were Christmas day. They chirped joyfully about all the things they could do with their new toy. Not even Zeke's insistent smacks could silence Dwight.

When the virgin cattle rustlers returned to their camp, of course, they did not quite know what to do with their prize. The Strongs could hardly take the cow with them on their adventures. Zeke had no idea how to milk a cow, nor butcher one. He had heard that there was money to be made from illicit cattle sales, but where would he sell the beast?

It was very late, and the hesitant sun was slowly blurring the purple gloom with grey dawn sunshine. Zeke was confronting the fact that, once again, he had done something very stupid indeed.

Charlie remembered his father as a hard man, a brawler and drinker. He would be violent to his sons when intoxicated or angry. Zeke thought nothing of going for days without washing nor eating, and expected his boys to follow his example. Yet Charlie recalled that his father was almost perpetually smiling and optimistic. Even when some drunk from the saloon had bloodied his nose over a trifle, Zeke would laugh the affair off. Despite being an unemployable idler, Zeke had always positively made the best of things.

Zeke had handed his rifle to his sons, and Charlie and Dwight had taken it in turn to shoot the cow to death. It had taken them a few tries before the defenceless animal toppled, but when the cow collapsed, it effected waves of laughter amongst the Strongs.

Remembering the comical bovine encounter, Charlie started laughing to himself in the saddle. Dwight joined in, too, though Dwight had no idea why.

When the Strongs were teenagers, they settled in a town named Gorse. Zeke had commandeered a derelict shack just outside of town. Nobody tried to chase them off. The Strongs were not worth the trouble.

Gorse was a rural community. At times, Zeke worked as a farmhand before his laziness and hot temper inevitably brought the employment to a heated conclusion. Their father had a pathological weakness for petty theft. At times, he would steal something useful like a wood stove, or food. Zeke would also thieve worthless and useless trinkets, purely for the joy of stealing.

The Strongs idled away their years. Sometimes, they would go for days and days without eating or bathing. The family rose from their makeshift beds whenever they felt like it. The Strongs did not keep regular hours. Through a combination of meagre earnings, plundered staples and charity from pitying townsfolk, the Strong family survived.

Zeke was a brute to anybody who said the wrong thing to him, or looked at him the wrong way. In Gorse, he was reputed as a hard-drinking layabout who neglected his sons. From time to time, Zeke did not come home to the shack, having been incarcerated in the jailhouse. Yet, Charlie remembered him as a kind and devoted father. While Zeke was hardly a disciplinarian, the only thing he could not abide was his sons fighting each other. In any scuffle between Charlie and Dwight, Zeke would drag them apart.

'You are the Strong brothers and you will not fight each other. We stick together, we three. Fight them, boys. Fight the rest of the world. But don't you dare fight each other!', he would insist in a voice that did not invite debate.

Zeke had also been relentlessly cheerful. Even when the Strongs were starving and stinking, he had remained positive.

'Don't worry, boys. I'll get you through this,' he would chirp. And he always did. Even when imprisoned in jail, he would set aside the thin gruel they served him. Zeke would take it home for his boys.

It was Zeke's misguided commitment to his sons that had led to his destruction. Growing into young men, Charlie and Dwight inherited a taste for robbery. The sheriff of Gorse had caught them shoplifting. They had been pathetically pocketing cans of soup, but theft was a crime and Charlie and Dwight were old enough for the jailhouse.

Tell of their arrest reached Zeke. To describe him as enraged would have been an understatement. His sons would have been released in a day or two, but that was too much for Zeke. Armed with a rifle he hardly knew how to operate, Zeke had marched into Gorse to initiate his jailbreak.

It was a bittersweet memory for Charlie. He vividly recalled cheering and whooping from the cell he shared with Dwight. Their own dad had burst into the sheriff's office and psychotically shot the town marshal dead. As Zeke frantically reloaded the carbine, the deputy had unholstered his own weapon. The lawman shot Zeke in the gut. Literally dying on his feet, Zeke returned fire and eliminated the deputy. He had now slaughtered all of Gorse's lawmen.

Impotently trying to stop the stream of blood from his

belly with a palm, Zeke had been in agony. With a bear's dedication to his cubs, his last energies had been sapped finding the jailhouse keys and unlocking his sons. He then collapsed.

'Get out of town, boys. And stick together.' Zeke had groaned his terminal words through clenched teeth before finally succumbing to the bullet.

The Strongs had fled. While Dwight's impetuosity could be a hindrance, the brothers had remained loyal to each other. Their long list of criminal outrages over the following years were, they felt, testament to their father's bravery.

Thinking back both saddened and gladdened Charlie. He was sorrowful that he had lost his father. Charlie was also extremely proud of Zeke's final courageous acts.

Charlie could see the same fraternal devotion amongst the Connors. He was a little disappointed that Adam seemed to be such a big baby, but Charlie would see what he could do about that. Nonetheless, his new and favoured son Bob was standing by his brother.

Towards the end of a frustrating day of hindered climbs and wobbly descents, the party at last made its final decline. Riding mindfully down the slippery rocky hill to the plains, Charlie could just about discern a black square on the horizon. John Morris' ranch.

CHAPTER 22

Dwight was particularly excited to be so near their destination. As the riders left the hills and returned to grassland, Dwight fired his Colt wildly into the air. He was shooting indiscriminately, causing the Connors to stiffen fearfully.

'That where we're headed?' Bob prodded Charlie, indicating the ranch on the horizon.

'Yes, son. It is,' Charlie responded. 'My friend will be most pleased to meet you.' Charlie was under orders to keep quiet about the plans for the Connors. Yet he could not resist hinting at something going on behind the scenes. Charlie thought that he was teasing Adam and Bob. In fact, Adam and Bob were only angered and frightened by Charlie's secrecy.

The plains were serene, basking in the orange pastel lights of sunset. There were gentle moos from cows contentedly grazing in the ranch's paddocks. Approaching the ranch, the party did not see any men. The only human sounds were Dwight's gleeful shrieks, if they could be described as human. Though the familiar scent of grass reminded the Connors of home, the pleasant smell did not relieve their fears. The Strongs seemed to be delighted that they were at their journey's end. Adam and Bob, however, pondered what ordeal awaited them in this mysterious ranch.

Bob unexpectedly halted his ride, forcing the others to stop as well. He scowled at Charlie.

'I am not going any further, Charlie. Are you going to ransom us, or what? My family don't have money. Whoever owns this ranch sure as heck does. I don't get it. What do you want?'

Charlie exhaled with false weariness, as if his errant son was testing his patience. His sighs were a pretence of exasperation, but inwardly Charlie was concerned. He had done as Morris had commanded, and now they were but miles from him. Charlie was unwilling to release his grip on the Connors when they were so close to the end.

'I'm taking you to the ranch, Bob. When we get there, my friend will explain everything.' Charlie's obfuscation further enraged Bob. While his bizarre abduction had perplexed him, Bob had been trying to guess what the Strongs' rationale could be. Not cash, for his father was not wealthy. Perhaps the Strongs had actually needed new recruits to their cause. However, the Wells robbery had been so ill-prepared.

'Your friend?' Bob doubted that Charlie had ever formed any kind of friendship. 'No, Charlie. I am not moving until you give me some answers.'

Charlie weighed up his next move. Dwight could sense that Bob was steadfast, and his eyes flickered nervously between Charlie and the Connors. Dwight began reloading his Colt.

Morris wanted the Connors alive. The Strongs had

been permitted to rough them up as far as necessary. Charlie had used threats and mild cruelty during the Connors' kidnapping. However, with Bob now emboldened thus, Charlie had an inkling that merely flashing his gun would be insufficient. He raised his voice.

'That's enough lip, Bob! Now come on – or you'll regret it!'

'No.'

Charlie withdrew his revolver and emphatically cocked the weapon with a loud click.

'Move it, Bob.'

'You don't have the guts, Charlie.' Bob had correctly judged that, for their own nefarious reasons, the Strongs would keep them alive. His brash defiance made his heartbeat quicken.

From his lair, Morris studied the confrontation amongst the riding party. Despite the dimming light and his great age, he possessed an eagle's vision. He had hired the Strongs many times. Though their methods were clumsy and slipshod, they had always delivered results. He could not hear the argument, but had guessed well enough what might be happening. Morris was not willing to let the Connors slip away when they were so close to his clutches.

The ranch was remote from Morriston. It was not truly part of his business operations. Though he farmed cattle here, the ranch was in fact a hideaway. The herd of cows was only for appearances. His ranch was managed by a skeleton crew of able men. While they were skilled cowpunchers, Morris' henchmen also boasted deadlier abilities.

Morris pulled the cord of the bell in his study. Moments later, Enrique entered the chamber. The thin, sullen Latino was Morris' de facto platoon sergeant. He, too, had been spying on the confrontation on the plains. Enrique half-expected that Morris would order an intervention.

Charlie was so frustrated that his face had reddened. Fond as he was of Bob, he was dearly tempted to terminate the dispute with a bullet. Dwight had joined Charlie in cajoling the Connors, but this contribution only irked Charlie further. Dwight was a loyal brother, but he did not really understand what the Strongs had been commanded to perform.

The thunder of scores of hoofs sang in the air, and Charlie's flesh tingled from the vibrations in the ground. Ten armed horsemen rode out from the ranch, and within moments the Strongs were surrounded. Charlie was backfooted, but relieved when he realized that they were Morris' men. In a well-practised manoeuvre, they formed a circle around the brothers, their rifles pointing inwards.

'Mr Morris sent us to give you a hand,' Enrique snorted. He had long disliked the Strongs, regarding them as unpredictable and unprofessional. Enrique was pleased to be able to show them up. This resentment was lost on the Strongs, who were hardly sensitive types. They were cheered that the awkward confrontation had been resolved.

'I've been ordered to look after the Connor boys. But Mr Morris didn't say nothing about you looking after the Strong brothers,' Enrique added.

Bob still suspected that he and Adam were needed alive. When Charlie and Dwight sagged in their saddles, dead under a salvo of bullets from Enrique and his men, he saw that the Strongs were not indispensable.

CHAPTER 23

Eli struggled through the mountain trail. It was a treacherous passage, and his horse neighed its resistance on every slippery undulation. The ride was worsened by Eli's poor concentration. During his manhunter days, his mind was always consumed by the chase. Today, though, he was distracted. Suzanne's revelations about Bob bothered him. Something else she said was also irking him. Suzanne had insisted that Eli had a pure heart. Back in Desolation, Eli had been too eager to return to his hunt to absorb her flattery. Presently, though, her words played over and over in his mind.

Eli reached a plateau on the mountain passage. He was reluctant to rest, but knew he needed to straighten his thoughts. Vegetation was sparse on the flint-grey rocks, but Eli found a tree to tie his mount to. The horse needed some repose as much as he did. A single, careless mistake on these deadly hills would be costly, or even fatal. Were Eli to break a bone, nobody would be coming to his rescue.

He leaned against a boulder, and sipped from his

canteen. Eli reached into his breast pocket for the discarded string tie. The garment was soft against his fingertips. Eli slumped down to sit on his behind, and remembered. Though it had been some twenty years, the memories were vivid.

Scott Glenn had not been particularly difficult to follow. Glenn had been a multiple murderer and thief. Eli had picked up his trail from Glenn's most recent crime. Glenn, like most criminals, had been stupid and careless. Eli's quarry had not known how to cover his tracks, and Eli had expertly followed them out onto the plains.

While Eli had been certain that he had not been far behind Glenn, he had found Glenn's movements unusual. Why was Glenn riding out to the grasslands? Eli had pursued Glenn's ill-concealed hoofprints out to a remote ranch.

Eli had thought it odd that a cattle farm should be situated so distant from any town. Suspicious that the ranchers were harbouring Glenn, Eli had pounded on the main door with one hand, and readied his Colt with the other. The door had been opened by a towering figure. The man's face had been as craggy as a cliff face. He may have been a very old man, but he had been lean and strongly built. His gloomy expression had suggested that he did not appreciate visitors.

'Partner,' Eli had politely entreated. 'I'm looking for this man.' Eli had shown the rancher the wanted poster, but he had not looked at it. 'I believe he is in the vicinity. Can you help me in any way?'

'I haven't seen him before. I can't help you.' Before Eli could draw breath for his next question, the door had been slammed shut. Eli had had much experience with liars, and his investigator's instinct had told him that the rancher's words were false.

Curiously, Eli had picked up Glenn's trail once more. Perhaps he had only stayed in the ranch for a short time, for Glenn had appeared to have ridden back out to the plains. Though it had been a long journey to Morriston, that was where Eli had caught up with Glenn before shooting him dead.

Eli took another slug of water. It was lukewarm and tasted somewhat leathery, but this did not trouble him. The jigsaw pieces in Eli's mind were connecting.

Eli had later learned that the lying rancher was John Morris. Seldom seen in the town he practically owned, Morris was a reclusive figure both revered and feared. Twenty years ago, Eli had found it odd that Morris' men had taken away Glenn's body. However, he had not brooded over it, for by then Eli was blissfully in love.

Something else bothered Eli: a detail that had been unimportant long ago but was now significant. When Eli and Cassie had walked down the aisle together on their wedding day, Morris had been sitting on a pew. The church had been packed, for Cassie and Eli had been a much-loved couple in Morriston. At that time, Eli had been so ecstatically joyful that he had not thought twice about Morris' presence. Recalling the event, his attendance now seemed portentous and menacing.

Of course, the first hymn during the wedding ceremony had been Pure Heart.

*

Eli was not given to temper tantrums, but he forced himself to his feet and hurled his canteen away in rage. The string tie. The apparent marriage in Beulah. Pure Heart.

'I'm such a fool!', he screamed into the empty mountain air. Morris had something to do with all this, and had been manipulating him from afar. Suzanne, too. Eli cursed his own weakness in confiding in her, and regretted his fleeting attraction. He suddenly wanted to throttle her until her eyes bulged. Eli had thought he was following the clues, but unseen hands had been guiding him.

Angry though he was, the realization had concentrated Eli's mind. He remounted, and continued along the hilly passage.

There was an unknown link between Eli and Morris. Eli guessed that it was something to do with Glenn. Yet it had been twenty years. And what did his sons have to do with it?

The final steps of the mountain trail were perilous, but Eli found he attacked them with much more self-control. Every slippery rise or fall of the black hillside took him a pace closer to his sons, and the truth.

Eli knew he was drawing nearer when he sensed the faint whiff of the grasslands. The skies were darkening, and already a handful of stars winked knowingly. He rested briefly atop the final ascent, before the declining path guided him back to the prairie. It was gloomy, but Eli's eyesight adapted well to the darkness.

He looked down at the grasslands looming below. Though it was shadowy, he could discern the black shapes of the farm buildings. Eli never thought he would return to the Morris ranch.

CHAPTER 24

Enrique and his men directed the Connors back towards the ranch. Adam and Bob were stunned. They did not understand the reasons for their abduction in the first place. Yet much as they loathed their captors, to witness them being gunned down so unexpectedly was shocking. The brothers were perplexed. Enrique's men took the reins of the Strongs' horses, leading them with the dead bodies still wilting in the saddles.

Enrique led them to a corral behind the main ranch-house. It was darkening now. The strange men surrounding the Connors muttered, some of them in Spanish. Though Adam and Bob could not follow the discourse, they could tell that it was not idle chatter. These men were lethal, ready to spring at the slightest sign of danger.

Sensing his guests' dumbstruck trepidation, Enrique turned back to them.

'We ain't like the Strongs, boys. We are gonna look after you. But you'll have to work for your keep. In fact, I've got a little job for you right now.'

The crew dismounted at the corral. They also removed

the swaying bodies of the Strongs from their rides, dropping them crudely on the grass. Enrique dismissed his men who returned inside. He lit a lamp, and approached the Connors. The lantern's yellow rays illuminated part of Enrique's stern face, leaving the rest masked by the ghostly blackness. Though Enrique was smiling glibly, his teeth appeared menacing under the fading light.

'You two – pick up Charlie Strong and follow me.'

'What?' Bob was flummoxed. 'Where are we going?'

'Just do as I say!' Enrique was typically softy spoken, but his words could snap into a snarl whenever he sniffed the slightest opposition.

The Connors obeyed. Bob hooked his arms under Charlie's lifeless shoulders, while Adam took his legs.

'I don't like this, Bob. What the heck is going on now?' Adam whispered, only to be shushed by Enrique. The Connors staggered after Enrique as he led them through the corral gate, up a gentle hill to what looked like a small cemetery. There were three spades laying on the ground there.

'Start digging,' Enrique commanded. Adam and Bob released Charlie unceremoniously, relieved to be unburdened. They did not feel any gladness that their abductor was no more. The brothers were in fact angry that, even in death, Charlie was bothering them.

Bob noted, as his foot pressed the diamond-shaped spade into the soft earth, that the shovels were brand new. The hard, steel teeth of the spades bit clean mouthfuls out of the soil, their strokes making groans as metal ground against the earth. Adam laboured arduously, for he was sapped. His confusion as to the odd events only magnified his fatigue. Bob was no less beat, but concentrated his simmering frustrations into every thrust of the shovel. He dug with vigour.

Enrique assisted them. When the improvised grave was deep enough for Charlie to be rolled in, Enrique halted the digging. With scornful, sharp, kicks, he pushed Charlie into the shallow pit. A burial place this slight would be irresistible to foxes and wolves. None of the three minded. As they patted down the soil on top of Charlie's inanimate, gawping face, Bob – despite the weird circumstances – felt great satisfaction. The thought of a wild animal's fangs tearing the lifeless skin from Charlie gladdened him.

As they gave Dwight the same treatment, Bob grew bolder, if not exactly relaxed. Digging the second hole, he peered around. There was a pattern of small headstones in rows over the hill. The darkness was now thickening. Squinting, Bob observed that almost all the gravestones bore the name Morris. There was only one with a different title: Scott Glenn.

'Sir,' Bob began, as politely as he could. 'Will you tell us what's happening? The Strongs wouldn't tell us a darn thing. Who's this friend of theirs?'

Before Enrique could answer, the rumble of another's thunderous tones made them turn their heads. Morris did not like to raise his voice, and he never needed to. His words carried through the air like the crash of waves. The three saw a silhouette of a man at the foot of the hill. So tall and strongly-built was the figure that, for a second, the Connors thought it might be a tree.

'You've been through a lot, young men, but now you are my guests. Follow me.'

They dared not disobey.

CHAPTER 25

The Morris family had been minor nobles in their native England. Once wealthy and powerful, they fled, penniless when Lord Morris had been hung for treason. They were amongst the first settlers in the new world. Though they arrived with little more than their suitcases, their sense of entitlement equalled their wickedness. Their peers in the West hunted in the woods, toiled in the fields and traded with the Indians. The Morrises, however, trod a lazier, easier pathway to affluence: murder.

Settlers would mysteriously fail to return to their cabins, which were swiftly annexed by the Morris clan. Though Wyoming was then a young territory and the population was sparse, whispers about the reclusive family with the snotty accents soon spread. Nobody dared refuse a Morris. During the following decades, the Morrises bought farms, ranches, land and businesses for bargain prices. The brave few who dared resist usually vanished mystifyingly.

There had been twenty Morrises when they first swooped on the Americas. Because they regarded their bloodline as superior, they were not willing to intermarry.

Before their disgrace in England, Lord Morris would have engineered bridges to other aristocrats through marriage.

Wyoming, however, lacked any suitable nobility. Cousins were wed to cousins. At times, Morriston women were forced into wedlock. These interlopers never lasted long. After they had borne children, these outsiders suspiciously disappeared. The sheriffs were but hand-picked stooges, and dared not investigate.

The effect of the Morris family's arrogant disdain for their lessers was that their numbers dwindled. John Morris had been an only child. His mother had been a local pauper, who – so it was said – died in childbirth. When John was born, he and his father were the only surviving Morrises.

The ranch where John was raised was a nursery for evil and madness. Forbidden from associating with other children, John grew up with little companionship. He was schooled by private tutors. Lacking friends or siblings, John found other, crueller recreations.

John's father had been cold and solitary. He had always been too busy to discipline or nurture young John. Without a guiding hand to address John's callous behaviour, John tired of cutting the throats of cats and dogs. Growing into a young man, John came to view his father's servants and cowboys as playthings. When John's barbaric treatment of a kitchen girl caused a stir at the ranch, John's father finally came to show an interest in him.

John had been summoned to his father's study. An ordinary boy would have trembled at the prospect of his father's wrath. John, though, had always lived without repercussion. The emotion of fear was unknown to him. He had been curious, though, as to what his father (who was nearly a stranger to him) desired.

John's father had leaned back in his expensive leather armchair. He had been puffing on his pipe, a glass of whiskey in one hand. Far from angry, he had been amused by his son's ruthlessness.

'John,' he had begun, in relaxed, pensive tones, 'it will not be long before I leave this world.' Indeed, John estimated that his father must have been at least fifty when he had sired him. 'Soon, you will be the only remaining Morris. I must begin to teach you how to conduct our affairs.' He had paused to puff on his pipe. 'Now firstly, keep your hands off the servants. I do not care for them any more than you do, but I don't want any fuss nor scandal. We Morrises keep our business secret from the rabble.'

'Yes, Father,' John had answered. He had been intrigued as to where this was leading.

'Now go to bed. We'll ride out early in the morning. Then your education will really begin.'

At dawn the next day, the Morrises and five heavies had ridden out to a new farmstead. The smallholding had been operating for hardly a year, but was earning a modest living for its owner. Unfortunately, the farmer had ignorantly omitted to pay tribute to his new master.

It had been so bright and sunny that day that John had had to shield his eyes from the sting of the sun. They had ridden up to the tiny house where the farmer had been milking a cow in his corral. The settler was a man with an honest face. John had been sickened by the man's stink: a reeking mix of milk and sweat. John's father, though, had smelled blood.

'Good morning, partner. Here to talk business. Come

to offer you a good price for a share of your farm.'

'Pardon me, sir. It's not for sale.'

At this point, Morris had stopped his pretence of politeness. Bellowing at the farmer, Morris had manhandled the settler back into his cabin. With five armed henchmen behind him, the dairyman did not fight back. John had followed them in. There, with the man's speechless wife and screaming children watching, the man had signed over the deeds to his property.

John had learned much that day. He had glimpsed a hitherto unknown plain of opportunity to be heartlessly plundered.

'Son,' his father had instructed during the ride home, 'if there's something you want, go and get it. If you can't get it, take it.'

His father's pitiless philosophy had been impressed on John. During the following years, John had learned that his father had been right. Nobody is going to defy a Morris. In manhood, John had continued his father's merciless ways.

John's father had been right about something else, as well. Not long after the brutal lesson at the smallholding, he had indeed left the mortal world. John had snuck into his father's bedroom and smothered him under a pillow.

John had also added to his father's business affairs. He had an ear for scandal, or weakness. John's father had been a fiend, but John learned how to manipulate his marionettes with favours and quiet words.

He had never lost his taste for viciousness, though. Leading the Connors into his ranch, John was keen to share his latest toy.

CHAPTER 26

'My name is John Morris, lads. I'm sure you must have heard of me.'

Of course, the Connors had. They had glimpsed him in town from time to time. Adam and Bob knew little of their host, though. He was always spoken of in hushed, reverential tones. Morris was leading them through his plush house. The recent days had been strange for the Connors, and visiting the Morris ranch was odder yet.

The buildings in Morriston tended to have a whiff of sawdust or wood. Morris's ranch, though, had a stinking, chemical scent. The house must have been scrubbed thoroughly and often with cleaning powder. It had obviously cost a lot of money to furnish the house. The whole place was like a museum. Morris decorated his mausoleum with stuffed animals, suits of armour, and crystal skulls. But for the scrape of their footsteps, the interior was hauntingly silent.

'Come with me, boys. Come with me.'

At their rear, Enrique was guarded. He was confident that he and his Colt could quell any coup by the Connors, yet he was not complacent. Enrique had spoken with his master's spies, and knew what the Connors were capable of. He had noticed Bob's furtive glances at him.

Enrique had no great warmth for Morris. His loyalty was akin to that of a professional soldier rather than a devout acolyte. Enrique drew great pride from his reputation. More than a cheap gunny, he was a fixer who never shied from a dirty job. Usually, Enrique carried out assassinations, or helped witnesses to remember (or forget) the truth with the correct degree of clarity. This time, though, he could not fathom his boss' scheme. His employer paid well enough, though, so Enrique had not debated the matter.

He had worked for Morris long enough to develop a sense for his moods. Morris typically delivered his orders without embellishment. He kept it simple, even when decreeing murder. Tonight, though, Enrique was finding Morris talkative and restless. It was not apparent to others, but Enrique detected differences in Morris' gestures and words. He was most pleased to be receiving his unwilling guests.

When they reached the door to the cellar, Morris turned to send him away.

'Enrique – leave us for now. Go outside and wait for our next guest. I'll look after the Connors.'

Enrique nodded his compliance and headed back outside. Morris preferred to leave the front line of his business to Enrique. He knew from experience, though, that Morris was not afraid of getting his hands dirtied – or bloodied. Morris could well handle the Connors.

The cellar door groaned as Morris opened it. Though his face was like a weathered tombstone, Bob thought he saw the faintest of smirks as Morris gestured for the brothers to follow him downstairs.

The basement's macabre gloom was dense, yet faintly illuminated by a lamp. Walking apprehensively behind Morris, the Connors thought they heard murmurs of pain from within the murk. Reaching the bottom of the steps, Bob's eyes had to adjust to the darkness. His mind also had to adapt to what he saw down there.

The cellar was large enough to make a fine vault for exotic wines. Yet it was not the cool of the cellar that made the Connors shiver. Above, Morris's bric-a-brac had been sinister. However, Bob had not expected him to hold a prisoner in his basement.

A wretched figure swung from manacles bolted to the wall. Though the chains were long enough for the captive to stand, the spectre was too weak to. Bob guessed that it was a young man, but only because the shape wore torn trousers and a ripped shirt. It was difficult to discern whether the apparition's face was darkened by shadows or bruising.

A wooden table rested in the centre of the dungeon, on which stood a porcelain jug of water. Morris took the vessel over to the prisoner, and poured it carefully over the wretch's broken lips. The water seemed to revive the captive, and he gulped mindlessly and desperately at the fluid.

Morris was ready to begin.

'As you know, boys, I own half the county. My men caught this man stealing from one of my stores – where he was being paid to mind the till. Instead of turning him over to the sheriff, though, I thought I'd entertain my guests.'

The Connors stiffened. Under the Strongs, the entertainment had not been wholesome. They did not like Morris' pregnant suggestion.

The brothers' uncomfortable shudders seemed to prompt Morris. From some niche hidden by the gloom, Morris conjured something. They could not make out what the artefact was. When Morris' arm arced violently, though, the Connors recognised the lightning snap of a bullwhip striking the ground.

Though plainly weakened by hunger and thirst, the prisoner was electrified by the weapon's callous crack. He forced himself to his feet. The wretch appeared to be imploring Morris. His disorientation and broken teeth warped the pleas into incomprehensible mumbles.

Morris looked to Bob, who fixed him back scornfully. Morris respected that: so few possessed the nerve to meet his penetrating gaze. His agents had reported back about Bob's flair for the criminal, and Morris was fascinated.

He handed the whip to Bob.

'Young man – give this fool a hiding. Don't hold back. I want you to enjoy every second.'

The wooden handle was warm and moist from Morris' grip, when Bob took it. Seizing the weapon, it was as if Bob was a valve in a steam train. He was charged with passionate energy which simply had to be expressed.

Adam recalled Bob's description of his feelings after shooting dead the overweight tough back in Desolation. Bob had been intoxicated, as if drunk with a lethal liquor. To Adam, his brother once again became a stranger as he gleefully struck blow after stinging blow on the wailing prisoner.

CHAPTER 27

Eli waited a little while. This was a challenge to his patience, for he was eager to storm the Morris ranch. Somewhere deep in his gut he knew that he was near to his sons. His father's instinct was reeled in by his man-hunter wiles, though. Eli had no idea how many men were guarding the ranch. He was well aware, though, that he was but a single man. Determined as he was, Eli forced himself to wait until the sun had fully retired.

Eli repeatedly looked up at the white orb. The antici-pation was almost painful. He made himself be patient. He would be unable to strike without the cover of dark-ness. It was as if the sun could sense Eli's keenness, and enjoyed observing him wait anxiously. As Eli hid behind a black rock, he frequently made impatient glances to monitor the sunset's unhurried progress. The plains were warming rods for the sun during the day. Yet, at night, with little cloud, the prairie skies cruelly sapped a man's heat. Eli shivered. The plains could be deadly cold after sundown. He drew his coat tight, but the garment did not help.

The Morris ranch was isolated. Twenty years ago, Eli

had found this unusual. Morris' purposeful distancing of himself from his town and his apparent subjects made more sense, now. The magnate ruled over his dominion from the shadows. Eli had no idea why Morris had abducted his sons, and wondered fearfully what secrets would be exposed tonight.

The farm's isolation made its surroundings unnaturally quiet. Even the cows were sleeping now, and not so much as a coyote sang to the stars. Eli would need to take measured, padded steps. Every single one of his movements would need to be controlled and silent. The still air would carry the merest whisper to the ears of unseen sentinels.

When Eli judged that the sun was sufficiently hidden, the manhunter set off. He left his ride tied to a black rock on the hills. With a wolf's stealth, Eli took calculated, controlled paces down the final descent from the hills to the grassland. It was perhaps a mile or two across the plains to the ranch. The approach would take less than thirty minutes if you were out for a brisk walk on a summer's day. For an expert tracker such as Eli, though, the advancement would be more meticulous.

Treading the soft ground, Eli was glad that the grass masked his footsteps. There were lights on in the ranch, and occasionally a shadow rushed past an illuminated window. Eli guessed that there were perhaps ten men in the farmhouse. Never had the bounty hunter fought against such overwhelming numbers. He would need subterfuge to outwit them, or else Eli's attack would be suicidal. Dangerous as his intrusion would be, his love for his sons compelled him to steel himself.

Eli took a deliberately meandering path up the gentle hill to the ranch. The windows brightened patches of the grassland, leaving other areas concealed by the gloom. It was within these shadowy pools that Eli secreted himself.

At the front gate to the ranch, Enrique was sentry for the night. He had sent his men to their beds. For some murky reason, Morris wanted as few as possible involved in his secret scheme. Enrique was happy to indulge his master. He was confident that he could manage Eli.

Guard duty was part of a mercenary's training. In his younger days, Enrique had spent so long as a sentry that he had cultivated an owl's night vision. He admired the skilful way that Eli was keeping to the shadows, and moving in such a silent manner. A lesser man than Enrique would have been deceived.

Nice try, Enrique thought. But you'll have to do better than that, Eli.

Feeling an arrogant compulsion to tempt Eli closer, Enrique leaned on the gate. He lit a thick cigar, doing nothing to conceal the flame from his match. Enrique drew deeply, making a show of exhaling as much smoke as possible. His demeanour was one of studied, pretended nonchalance.

The red wink of the match and the aroma of the expensive cigar were not lost on Eli.

I can handle this guy, he thought. The guard looks half asleep.

Eli arced in the darkness to a point further along the perimeter wall. He planned to inch across and overpower the sentry. The ranch was bounded by a waist-high stone wall. Reaching the barrier, Eli descended to his hands and knees. He would crawl along the wall unseen and unheard, and then pounce.

Enrique continued to pretend to stare into space,

absorbed by nothing but his smoke. He had watched Eli sneak over to the wall, and continued to observe him in the periphery of his vision. Enrique respected Eli's guile – but he was not fooled. Indeed, as Eli neared, Enrique had to suppress an amused smirk.

Eli rose, cocking and pointing his Colt in a single, seamless motion.

'Freeze,' he spat through gritted teeth. 'Give me your weapon, and put your hands up, or there's going to be trouble. Real bad trouble.'

Enrique's laughter unnerved Eli, and he tightened his grip on his revolver.

'What's so funny, partner?'

Eli resented the guard's smug manner of removing his gun-belt, and handing it over arrogantly. He could tell that this guard was more than some lazy retainer who drew sentry duty tonight. Enrique was not fazed in the slightest by the Colt in his face. Though he was now unarmed and outgunned, Eli could tell that this man had deadly potential.

'Mr Connor – there's really no need for all this cloak and dagger. I'm not going to hurt you. In fact, Mr Morris has been expecting you.'

Eli half-expected as much. The kidnapping of his sons had led to one question after another. The sentry's unanticipated reaction was merely another piece of the jigsaw.

'Where are my sons?'

'Follow me up, Mr Connor. My boss will explain everything.'

CHAPTER 28

Suzanne's concentration was absent. Her saloon was not as raucous tonight. Perhaps the entertainment supplied by the Connors had been ample excitement for a few evenings. More likely, though, was that the kind of hoodlums who were drawn to Desolation – as flies are magnetised by dung – had already squandered their plundered pittances.

Perhaps a dozen men sat around the bar-room. The lack of cigar smoke this evening meant that the faint, sickly blend of stale beer and decay could not be masked. Suzanne was fastidious when it came to cleaning her saloon. Nevertheless, there was always an undercurrent of corruption in the rotten air which she could never, ever purge.

From behind the bar, Suzanne leaned forward on the counter. She rested her chin on her palms. Candy and Jezebel, when they thought Suzanne was not looking, pointed and giggled at their mistress. The scarlet ladies were enjoying a rare night of repose. While they had dressed and applied their makeup as usual, there was no trade tonight. They sat at the table and chattered. The harlots seemed to be the only ones who were not bored.

While the courtesans had the greatest admiration for Suzanne, it amused them to see her looking so far-away. Suzanne was their paymaster, bodyguard and surrogate elder sister. She demanded a hard night's work from them. Suzanne would not tolerate her courtesans resting on their butts when they could be on their backs. Yet she paid well and led by example. It was odd to see her so distant, like a child daydreaming through a tedious Latin lesson.

Suzanne would have enjoyed being bored. However, her mind was not seeking an escape from tedium. Rather, it repeated the same thoughts of Morris and Eli over and over. Suzanne could not comprehend Morris' plan. During their long association, she had never confronted nor questioned him. Suzanne had never been one to kowtow to men, yet Morris' mere presence made her bow her head fearfully. Her benefactor had honoured Suzanne's secret, and demanded little in return. Of course, she had looked the other way when Enrique and his heavies had shamelessly and overtly dragged men out of her saloon. This had not tested her conscience. Fights and killings were hardly rare in her bar. The louts that perished would not be missed – not even by their families.

This time, Morris was orchestrating a darker, deadlier ploy. Suzanne was doing something worse than pretending to forget one of Morris' tactical assassinations. What, though? Adam and Bob were barely on the cusp of manhood. Before their sickening corruption at the claws of the Strongs, they had had time and opportunity to walk an honourable path. Perhaps they still could. What could Morris want with these two young men?

Suzanne was also troubled by her treatment of Eli. While she had been raised in a house of harlots and now presided over a den for the dishonest, Suzanne was no deceptress. As a girl, a preacher had told her that she could not hide her light under a bushel. Suzanne had not exactly become very saintly, but the clergyman's words had stuck with her. In Suzanne's case, she could never conceal her inner fire.

Yet her deceit had snared Eli. Complicit in Morris' deception, she had guided him towards . . . towards what? That mountain trail was deadly enough in its own right. It pained Suzanne to imagine what awaited in Morris' prairie lair.

'Gimme a whiskey, Suzanne.'

The whole bar turned their heads when Suzanne yelped in surprise. So rapt had she been in broodiness that the customer's approach had startled her.

'Coming up, honey.' The boozer before her was an attractive, stocky man boasting a rich, black beard, inky curls and copper eyes. Suzanne could not recall the customer's name, but she had heard the whispers. Some said that brown-eyes forced himself on women. There was definitely something dubious about him. He was good-looking and charming – but he made Suzanne uneasy.

'Something on your mind, Suzanne? You're a little jumpy this eve.'

'Here's your drink, sweetie.' Suzanne slid the glass over, and the vessel scraped awkwardly on the wooden counter. She found it difficult to restrain her distaste.

Suzanne watched the dark drinker as he walked over to Candy and Jezebel. He was not quite drunk, but Suzanne could tell that he had already knocked back a couple of whiskies. The painted ladies chirped joyfully when brown-eyes sat on their table. Candy and Jezebel concealed their disgust well.

Suzanne tried to eavesdrop. She did not know if the rumours were true, but brown-eyes had an aura of evil. He was softly-spoken, yet boastful. Suzanne picked up snippets of his claims. The harlots skilfully faked rapture as he described beauties he had seduced, lawmen he had slain, and riches he had hidden away.

A patron could pay a fair price for some private time with Candy and Jezebel. Brown-eyes vainly felt that he was above that, as his paws grasped at the courtesans' comely curves. The harlots expertly fended him off with playful, yet firm, smacks. Suzanne watched with protective eyes, waiting to see if she should intervene. Her arbitration was unnecessary, though, for she had trained Candy and Jezebel well.

Brown-eyes lay his hand on Candy's knee. She brushed it away. When the customer tried putting his hand up her skirt, Candy sprang.

She scratched at his cheeks with her long nails. They broke his skin, drawing blood.

Jezebel, meanwhile, grabbed fistfuls of the assailant's long hair. She wrestled his head back as Candy continued to claw at his face.

Brown-eyes cried out in pain. He looked truly pathetic as he blindly tore at the air. There was laughter from the other customers, and a whimper from brown-eyes, as the painted ladies ejected him from the saloon. He would never return.

'You all right, ladies?' Suzanne approached them, not

doubting that her courtesans were intact.

'Yes, ma'am. We're one hundred per cent OK. You taught us good, Suzanne.' Candy was unshaken, even a little proud.

'That fellow was rotten,' Jezebel added. 'No woman can bend to a creep like that.'

On hearing Jezebel's words, Suzanne instantly knew what she had to do.

CHAPTER 29

When Bob had thrashed the prisoner so violently that he was too exhausted to swing the whip one more time, he rested. Flailing the weapon had been intoxicating, but bent over panting, the first fingers of guilt pressed on his shoulders. Bob could not bear to look at the captive, whose breathing was now so shallow that it was inaudible. Nor could he face Adam, who scarcely recognised his older brother.

Morris was pleased, though. 'My informants were correct, Bob. You do have the touch of the outlaw about you.'

Bob resented this insinuation with venom, but only because he feared that it was right.

Morris unholstered his Colt, and cocked it. 'Now, let's go back upstairs. My next guest should be here by now.'

He directed them back through his macabre museum to his upstairs study. There, Eli had his gun trained on Enrique. The mercenary's flippant, elusive answers to Eli's interrogation were frustrating him. Eli

137

forgot this impotent rage the second his sons entered the chamber.

Neither Enrique nor Morris prevented Eli from rushing over to Adam and Bob and pressing them tight to his breast. For a few moments, Eli did not care for the danger they were in, nor whatever wrongdoings his sons may have been involved in. Holding his sons close was all that mattered.

Enrique had never indulged in compassion. Of course, he had not been stupid enough to hand his last weapon over to Eli. Enrique removed the Derringer he'd secreted in his leather boot.

'That's enough happy families,' Enrique barked. 'Split up! I said split up, darn it!'

Still holding his weapon, Eli broke the embrace. Enrique looked to Morris.

'Boss?'

He had followed his master's instructions without quibble. Now, though, it was over to Morris. Enrique, too, was curious to learn his boss' rationale.

Morris grinned broadly. It was unlike him to display any human emotion. The rancher walked over to his desk and poured himself a brandy.

'So, what's going on?' Eli insisted, raising his gun arm to emphasise his demand.

Morris sat back in his chair. Enrique had never seen him so relaxed, and he took this to be a bad omen.

'I am the last of the Morris family. We have always been particular about who we marry, or lay with. We had to preserve our blue blood. The Morrises hated to dilute it with the slime that runs through your veins.'

He took a sip of brandy, savouring it. It would be his

last ever drink.

'After my father died, I didn't much care for starting a family. I have enjoyed plenty of wicked women, but all I cared for was myself. I did not want a screaming infant ruining my fun.'

Morris began playfully cocking and uncocking his Colt. 'Well, I was wrong. When the letter came I could hardly believe it. I had fathered a son through some trollop. My way of looking at the world changed in a second. I'm a cruel man, no doubt. And selfish. For the first and only time, I felt love for another.'

A bullet of salty perspiration swam down Enrique's face to his lips. It was so unlike Morris to be so intimate, and it made him nervous.

'His mother was no good. She just wanted money out of me – which I gave her. Then, she wanted more and more. She was a poor mother to Scott. In the end, I got rid of her.'

'Scott Glenn,' Eli added. The circumstances now made a little more sense.

'Right. He never took my name, much as I insisted. Scott was unruly, troubled. The likes of you, Eli, would have called him a no-good bum. I raised him alone for a time, but Scott was . . . a naughty boy. Fighting, drinking. I sent him to boarding-school for a while, but he ran away.

'Then, as a man, he came to your attention, Eli. Scott killed several men over lord-knows-what. He rode back here. I urged him to stay, to hide. I could pay off the lawmen and judges. But Scott only stole some money and rode in to Morriston to get drunk.'

For a second, Morris seemed despondent. 'Scott was not . . . very smart.'

'You're right, Morris. Scott Glenn was a worthless, drunken crook. And I shot him. Why not kill me? Why not,' Eli gulped, 'kill my sons?'

Morris laughed callously.

'I'll kill you in a minute, Eli. But I wanted to do something much worse to your sons. The Strongs took them on some real adventures. Whiskey, women, theft, and – oh yes – killing. Your boys are killers now, Eli. They've tasted blood. In fact, Bob just gave an associate of mine a real nice whipping.

'In my own way, I have killed your sons. That is my revenge. Their hearts may beat, and their lungs may breathe. But inside, their souls are dead.'

Morris' eyes flashed with menace as he soared to his feet. 'Your sons are just like me.'

The finger on Eli's trigger had oozed a film of hot sweat. So angry was Eli that he trembled, and was dearly tempted to pull the trigger.

'So, you've been playing a stupid game with me right from the start!'

Morris knocked back the rest of his brandy. 'Cheers.'

Enrique was intrigued by the story. He admired Morris' touch of evil, but was anxious to conclude this silly outing. Perhaps next week he could return to beating up witnesses. Morris sensed his lieutenant's impatience, and nodded to Enrique.

The Derringer was a small handgun, and Enrique cared to avoid any mess. There was a gentle click as his thumb pulled back the little hammer.

Ever on high alert, Enrique paused as the music of gunfire played in the floor below. Quick-thinking as he was, Enrique was startled as Suzanne burst into the study.

She stank of gunpowder, and her eyes were burning fero-
ciously. And why was she holding a revolver?

CHAPTER 30

Suzanne had blustered blindly through the darkness. She had never ridden the deadly mountain path, but had no time to ask directions nor check the map. Suzanne had rocketed through the gloom almost suicidally. By the time she found her way to the grassland, and the Morris ranch, the hoofs of her steed were ruined. Her horse was beat, but Suzanne had not even started.

She had never visited her poison patron's farm, but tonight she had no taste for a guided tour. Suzanne knew that Morris' men could be watching her approach.

Let them watch, she thought. Stop me if you can.

Suzanne had two Colts in the holster around her waist. Both were fully loaded. She was handy with a gun, but no markswoman. However, Suzanne was not ruled by logic. Rather, her blood burned in her veins while an inferno blazed in her gut. She had never hurt a man that did not deserve it, nor wronged another. Her acquiescence to Morris had been shameful. Suzanne prayed that she had time to right the situation, and purge her dirtied conscience.

She found the main door unlocked. Sure enough, as Suzanne slammed the portal open, one of Morris' men was ready for her. She vaguely recognised him, until one of her bullets distorted his face horrifically. He plunged to the ground, dead. Though his lifeless finger rested on the trigger of his gun, Suzanne had been too rapid. She was hardly eliminating her opponents methodically. Suzanne was nothing but animal instinct, striking with dumb – yet deadly – luck.

She heard voices upstairs, and headed towards them. As she ascended the stairs, another unfortunate ran towards her. Suzanne made a bloodied hole in his chest before he even raised his gun arm. She sidestepped the gunman's toppling cadaver as he fell forwards down the stairs.

So resolved to rescue the Connors was Suzanne that she was feverish. Her crazed determination bordered on bloodlust. Suzanne was not thinking – only acting. When she entered the study, Suzanne noted that Eli, Morris and Enrique were armed. Without pausing to debate the tactics of such a confrontation, Suzanne aimed and fired at Enrique. The mercenary's last expression was one of puzzlement as he slumped to his knees, a bullet in his brain.

Morris wanted Adam and Bob to live out their days as monsters. He was certain that they would forever recall their experiences with shame, or else advance to worse cruelties and lawlessness. Whichever, now that his sons were eternally tainted, Eli could be dispensed with. Before Eli could react, Morris aimed at Eli's torso and pulled the trigger.

Eli collapsed, but his tortured cries signalled that he

was alive. Morris had missed his target. The bullet had torn its way through his shoulder. Adam and Bob hurried to his side.

The incapacitation of Eli did nothing to quell Suzanne's frenzy. Regarding Morris with spiteful contempt, she turned her Colt on him. Despite his great age, Suzanne had once found Morris to be an intimidating figure. Presently, though, he was pathetically trying to pull back the hammer on his handgun for another shot. Perhaps unsettled, or distracted by Eli's agonised groans, he struggled with shaking hands to cock the weapon once more. Morris was nothing but a weak, elderly man, but his condition did not arouse Suzanne's pity. Her disdain only swelled.

Though Morris' handling of the Colt was clumsy, it would only take him a few seconds to ready the weapon. Her senses heightened by the peril to intense awareness, those instants gave Suzanne ample time to cock her own revolver.

Her ears rang after she clenched the Colt's fiery metal. Suzanne's already sore wrist ached a little more under the frissons of the recoil. The air was so thick with cordite that it seemed to cling like a film of dirt to her flesh. Suzanne's bullet had penetrated Morris' core.

Innately, the rancher knew that these moments were his last. The pain was beyond excruciating, yet Morris' soul was a deep sea of hatred and cruelty. He looked down at his chest, and with his free hand dipped his fingertips in the blood leaking from the midriff. Morris examined his bloodied digits. He noted that they were tinged blue.

'So, I do have blue blood after all,' he croaked.

To Suzanne and the Connors, it was surreal. A bullet in his breast, Morris was steadfastly clinging to his life. He seemed to be literally dead on his feet. Morris, though the pain was nearly paralysing, viewed the situation with serene clarity. His limbs stiff, Morris lurched toward Suzanne, fighting to raise his frozen gun hand.

Suzanne gasped. Infirm though he had seemed, Morris' sheer bloody-mindedness made him inhumanly strong. She cocked her Colt to fire again, but somebody else was faster.

Morris' head slanted violently to one side as the report of another gunshot rang out. The rancher flailed almost drunkenly before finally collapsing.

Adam stood with his father's Colt held in his two hands thrust before him. Wisps of smoke rose from the weapon. The gun looked enormous in Adam's grasp: he was much slighter than his brother. Back in Desolation, he had seemed so meek compared to Bob. Suzanne saw none of that timidity now. Lethal resolve shone through Adam's eyes. Indeed, so resolute was Adam's gaze that Suzanne was taken aback.

Ever the sensible older brother, Bob led the survivors. His father continued to wail. The bullet had mercifully cut clean through. Bob cleaned and tied the wound, and helped his father to his feet. Suzanne put a comforting arm around Adam and guided him away from the bloodshed in the study.

There was no resistance from Morris' men as they returned to their rides. On hearing the gunfire, the remaining heavies had scurried away fearfully.

In the black flux between the mortal world and Hell, Morris was not certain whether he was thinking, dreaming, or something else as he slipped away. His final thoughts were that Adam, too, was infected by his wickedness.

CHAPTER 31

His teeth gritted, Eli had led Suzanne and his sons back to Morriston. Bob had done a good job of dressing his injured shoulder, yet the wound continued to throb. Despite the pain, Eli dug deep and rode on. He was with his sons once more, and they needed their father's leadership.

Returning home, it seemed like they had been away for many years. His sons had indeed aged considerably in that short time, but that was not something Eli cared to dwell on. At the Connor house, the four plunged into black, sleepy, pits.

At dawn the next day, it caused much comment when the Connor General Store was open for business. His arm in a sling, Eli inched around his shop, frequently closing his eyes in pain. It would have been prudent to rest for a time, but Eli was determined to impose his will on his weakened body. He could not help smirking in amusement as he served his curious customers. The store did a lot of business that day. Of course, by then, the Morriston townsfolk had heard all the rumours. They could not resist dropping in for a peek at the father of two outlaws, who was nursing his own gunshot wound.

Eventually, Sheriff Lee dropped in. Lee was dreading this confrontation. The ostensible lawman did not know the details, but Eli had ridden out alone a few days ago, returning with his sons and a bullet in his shoulder. Lee also knew that Morris had something to do with it all.

It did not please Eli to recount his ordeal. He was deliberately vague when it came to his sons' violent acts. Lee was relieved, yet rudderless. Morris had long been a silent threat, but Lee did not quite know what to do next.

'Ride up to his secret ranch, Sheriff. There's quite a few dead bodies up there, and some poor sap tied up in the basement. Clean that mess up. You can talk to my boys when they're ready.'

Lee acted on Eli's suggestion. The sheriff's deputies gave Morris a brief funeral in his private cemetery, and arranged for the interment of the dead thugs in boot hill. They took the prisoner, barely breathing, to the doctor.

Lee later spoke to Adam and Bob. The Connors' eyes were sunken, and their eye-sockets blackened as if dirtied by soot. He interrogated them in the presence of Suzanne and Eli, who made sure that the young men did not say too much. Their testimony was shocking, but the trail of cadavers emphasised its veracity. Had the sheriff pressed them, he could have exposed a number of inconsistencies in their explanation. Lee was stunned by the extraordinary events, though, and decided to leave restful hounds to their repose.

Eli allowed Adam and Bob to recuperate. It took weeks, but Adam's strength recovered. With his renewed vigour came a return of the familiar cheek and boisterousness. Suzanne stayed at the Connor house, and watched over their healing. She never thought that she would find herself mothering two young men in this way. At first, she felt melancholy to see Adam and Bob sleeping-in until midday, scarcely eating and trudging around the house like mummies. Suzanne was patient, though. She cooked and cleaned for her new flock, and chattered pleasantly about nothing. Never did she probe deeply about the fearful experiences they had shared.

Her patience and attentions were rewarded. Adam soon came to enjoy teasing Suzanne, and she was a playful foil to his jokes. She had sharpened her wit with years of ironic comebacks to the barbs of her customers in Desolation. When Adam returned to health, though, she found his constant cheek a touch tiresome. Fond as Suzanne had grown, she felt a little relieved when Adam returned to full-time work in the store.

Adam and Bob were old enough to understand what was happening between Suzanne and their father. While they still missed their dear mother, they approved. Adam and Bob made no comment when Suzanne advanced from her bedroll in the lounge to their father's bedroom. Even after the loss of Cassie, Eli had never been a forlorn man. He had drawn pride from his fine sons, and enjoyment from his successful business. Nonetheless, Adam and Bob noticed a certain joyful energy about him since Suzanne started sharing his life.

Two weeks before, Eli had been an unremarkable widower and shopkeeper, and father to two nice, young men. The Connor household had now been transformed into a hotbed of scandal. Suzanne cared nothing for the mores of Morriston's small-minded. Even though she loved her new family passionately, there was no rush to get married. Talk of Suzanne's former career reached the ears of Morriston's gossips faster than the Pony Express. The blabbermouths gleefully added to the rumours. Suzanne was also a Turkish heiress, or a Tartar sorceress, depending who you spoke to.

Morriston's prudes never said anything impolite to the faces of the Connors, though. Suzanne was living sinfully with the bounty hunter who exposed Morris, and was stepmother to two outlaws. Indeed, Sheriff Lee was retiring soon. Whenever Eli was asked whether he would be the next town marshal, his answer was tantalising: 'I'll think about it.'

At their dinner table, the Connors commonly roared with laughter when somebody shared the latest dumb rumour about them. The experiences they had shared were horrific, but those were in the past. Their present, and future, were promising.

Bob, though, was recovering at a slower pace. Physically he was well and had also returned to work at the store. He had, until the Strongs clawed him away, been courteous and retiring. The customers at the store could not detect the change in him. They were pleased (despite the rumours) to see the polite, young gentleman back behind the counter. Eli and Suzanne were worried, though. While Bob was the quiet one, he now passed hours in pensive silence. He had never been as outgoing as Adam, but had taken to going for long, solitary walks.

The Connors were hopeful, but something was continuing to trouble Bob.

CHAPTER 32

The warmth in the house was stifling. Bob was idling his Saturday afternoon. Adam was out riding, while Eli and Suzanne were shopping in town. Bob gazed out of the lounge window. Though indoors, he felt like an outsider looking in. Bob had frequently felt like this, lately.

The sky was an inviting, icy blue. The heat inside was bothering Bob. Suzanne made sure that their home was always spotless, but the balminess teased a mustiness from the woodwork. The occasional, cool gust of wind was like a distant siren call. Bob felt suffocated and decided to go for a long walk.

Before leaving the house, Bob strapped his rifle to his back. Even before Bob's abduction, his father had forbidden him from playing with guns. Since Bob's return, Eli had been particularly strict about locking his gun cabinet. Eli always kept the keys on his person. When unobserved, Bob had taught himself how to pick the lock. Before riding with the Strongs, Bob had not much cared for shooting. During his prolonged silences, it was now all he thought about. Perhaps because he was so quiet, nobody noticed Bob's furtive loans of the carbine. He always

returned the weapon unsuspected. Not so long ago, illic-
itly borrowing the weapon would have filled Bob with
guilt.

Guilt, Bob thought to himself as he set off on foot.
What is guilt? Bob had felt shameful following the
Strongs' bungled bank robbery. Yet he also felt a touch of
pride for his leadership. Bob was not certain whether he
was ashamed of his role, or ashamed that he was secretly
proud of himself.

Bob, at least intellectually, knew that it was wrong to
kill. After shooting the provocateur in Desolation,
though, Bob's spirit had soared like an eagle. He would
gladly have shot another, then another. Only Adam's terrified, confused eyes dragged him back to Earth. His
brother's reaction had made Bob's act all too real. It had
not been a daydream.

Such thoughts had been thrashing like stormy seas in
Bob's head. Returning home and getting back to work
had made Bob question the truth of what had happened.
Sometimes, it seemed as if another person had been kidnapped by the Strongs. It was almost like remembering a
dream.

Bob ascended the gentle hill overlooking Morriston,
although he did not realize that he was. So profound was
Bob's introspection, that his legs motored independently
of his mind. At the peak of the hill, Bob paused. He wondered for a second how he had arrived there, remarking
for a moment that he had been strolling for a while.

Looking down on Morriston as if he were a giant, Bob
noted that the town was still busy. Certain shops were still
open, and the numbers in the saloons were beginning to
swell. The townsfolk, from Bob's vantage point, were as

tiny as flecks of dirt. He was reminded of a flea circus. The air on the hilltop was fresh, and Bob savoured it. Morriston's farms and ranches were mostly quite distant from the main town. But for the odd baa or moo, Bob could hear only the whoosh of wind. He seemed to be paying special attention to sounds and smells lately. It was as though his senses had sharpened, or perhaps external noise merely echoed in the dark hollow of his soul.

Bob set off again. Half of him was concerned to return the rifle before Eli discovered its absence; the other half brazenly did not care. Bob's walk was aimless. He meandered mindlessly for miles. His pace was brisk, though, as if he were a yacht adrift guided by a powerful wind.

The faint reek of dung, and the snorts of horses, told Bob that he had reached the outskirts of a neighbouring farm. He approached the corral fence and watched the animals within, circling aimlessly. Horses are powerful beasts, and Bob recalled staring at them in frightened fascination as a child. As he gazed at the animals, Bob's mind returned to visions of the past weeks.

It was as though Bob's thoughts and sentiments were so ugly that he had to get away from the house before he could dwell on them. Bob irrationally imagined that his family could somehow see the hideous pictures in his head.

Unconsciously, Bob was grinning. His memory of the assault on Morris' prisoner was sweetly visceral. Bob had thrown stroke after stroke with the bullwhip, only desisting when he was too breathless to hurl another. His victim's pathetic whimpers had only encouraged him.

It was solely in these private moments that Bob was truthful with himself. His love and protectiveness of his family had not faded. He had hated and feared the Strongs and Morris. The addictive thrill of crime, of snatching another's life could not be denied, though. Inwardly, Bob had been building on his memories with violent and wicked fantasies of his invention. Though it troubled him, he was beginning to understand the allure of lawlessness.

It seemed that Morris had succeeded. Bob had been infected with his sadistic sickness.

Further along from the corral was the farmhouse. Within, the farmer was washing up before dinner with his family. Leaning over the washbowl, he looked out of his window. There, he spotted Bob standing at his corral. Again. The farmer did not mind. He had heard what Bob had been through. Bob had been showing up at his farm frequently. The young man always seemed entranced, as if he had been sleepwalking for miles. This time, the farmer thought he would say hello.

'Howdy,' he beckoned, stepping outside. 'Bob Connor, isn't it?'

The greeting startled Bob. He was flustered, but then replied.

'Yes, sir. How are you doing?'

Bob seemed uncomfortable, almost as if he had been caught doing something he should not have.

'Would you like to come in? We're about to have supper. Join us.'

The farmer had a walrus moustache to match his walrus physique, but his great strength could not disguise his palpable kindness. His welcome made Bob feel disgusted by his broodiness. This man was opening his home to Bob, yet here he was imagining unspeakable things.

'No thanks, sir. I'll be heading off.'

The farmer shrugged. He would never know what Bob had endured, and was keen to keep it that way.

Since returning home, there had been a constant division in Bob's mind. His memories of his violent acts sat in one compartment; the decency and bravery shown by Eli, Adam and Suzanne in another. Bob was not convinced that he was worthy of their devotion.

He carried on walking, until he was deliberately lost. The temptations he had surrendered to under Morris and the Strongs had been filthy. Bob had learned something, though. He had more nerve than he thought. He would now need to draw on that untapped fearlessness.

He had to lay down in rather an awkward position. Bob took the barrel of his rifle between his lips, and closed his eyes.

EPILOGUE

Candy and Jezebel had taken the lead when Suzanne had rushed out that evening, never to return. Suzanne was most certainly hot-tempered and fickle, but the painted ladies never imagined that Suzanne would desert them. When days turned into weeks, and tell of Morris' odd demise reached Desolation, the harlots realized that Suzanne was not coming back. They were surprised rather than angry. Suzanne had been a fine mistress. She had taken such pride in managing the saloon that it was astonishing that she should abandon it so easily.

When the letter from Suzanne finally arrived months later, signing over the bar to Candy and Jezebel, they had their final answer. Of course, Morris had been the true owner of the saloon, but he could not meddle from his roughshod grave. There was no pretender to the courtesans' property title.

After Suzanne's amazing departure, Candy and Jezebel were the only women left in Desolation. At first, the absence of Suzanne's protection unsettled the scarlet ladies. The escorts had been able apprentices under Suzanne, though. She had correctly predicted that they could handle the worthless bums that wafted in and out of Desolation.

The first change they made was their retirement as harlots. Skilled though they were in the bedroom arts, Candy and Jezebel directed their energies into managing their new business. Their old customers moaned obscene protests on learning that their indecent urges would not be indulged. Chloe and Jessica (their real names) were unmoved.

'Too bad, mister,' they would answer. 'We're business-women now. Another drink?'

The saloon ladies were, in any case, too busy with their new profession to practise the oldest profession. Perhaps because their baser lusts went unsatisfied, the bar's crooked clientele drank more. Serving whiskies, throwing out drunks, getting rid of dead bodies, breaking up fights and counting the overflowing takings consumed all of Chloe and Jessica's time. They had little opportunity to spend their monies. There was no bank in Desolation, but the safe in the saloon's office was bursting with cash. Even without the murderous talons of Morris directing his minions, Desolation remained a popular hiding place for hoodlums on the run.

This went on for many months. Season followed season.

Soon, thick snows smothered the heat from the scorching rocks. It was during a snowstorm that a stranger rode into Desolation.

The falling snow outside was stinging in its wintriness. It was positively painful to brave the cutting spears of precipitation hurled by the greyed skies. Though the grim billows in the heavens had swallowed the sun, the reflection of light by the snows was blinding. So frigid was the air that merely inhaling it bit the outsider's maw. The howl of the wind and the dazzle of the ground was befuddling. It was this confusion that arrested the visitor's progress, almost as much as the slimy snows.

Such wintry obstacles did not deter the traveller, for mere snow would not slow his quarry, either. Desperate men would not be halted by the weather. Fraught though the stranger's target might be, he was still a stupid criminal. The prey may have thought that the snows would cover his tracks. Indeed, the storm had obscured his trail somewhat, but the manhunter was ten steps ahead. His game, as predicted, had fled to Desolation, as he had done so many times in the past.

Desolation was not famed for its hospitality, but the stranger was gladdened to see the lights on in the saloon. The outsider followed the glowing orange beacon along the trail into town. Though he did not speak a word as he entered the bar, the traveller's mere physical presence announced itself.

Chloe was behind the counter that night. Despite her former career, she had not lost her eye for a handsome man. And my oh my, was this stranger something! He was as burly as a wrestler, and his smouldering eyes seemed to be scanning the entire room. Though dirty snows clung to his poncho, and his chin was smattered with black stubble, his unkemptness only added to his coarse charm.

Chloe rushed over to the attractive newcomer.

'What'll it be, mister?' she piped flirtatiously.

'Just a coffee, please, Candy.'

'Comin' up.' So, you remember my stage name? she thought. You're not such a stranger after all.

Bob knew that using Candy's name might reveal

himself, but he did not care. His quarry was sitting alone at a table, so drunk that he was nodding off: Harry Charles, wanted dead or alive, $150 reward. Bob knew what Charles looked like, but Charles did not know that Bob was chasing him.

It had been over a year since the farmer had found Bob stupidly turning the rifle on himself. Kind though the farmer undoubtedly was, he had been angered by Bob's erratic behaviour. The farmer had snatched the weapon away, and chased Bob off. When he had omitted to return the rifle to his father's cabinet, it had created a stir. It did not take long before Eli had learned from the farmer what Bob had been caught doing.

The incident had caused angered voices and distressed tears in the Connor house. Yet, it had been cathartic. The confrontations ended Bob's dark, yet self-pitying, meditativeness. Bob had also admitted a truth to himself. Morris had implanted a seed of barbarity in him, and Bob was addicted to the thrill of violence. By then, Eli could no longer conceal his own bloodied history. Bob had been both intrigued and inspired by his father's murky past. Perhaps Bob could channel his ferocity into something positive. He certainly had the brains to be a manhunter.

Bob was not yet twenty-one, yet his reputation as a fledgling tracker was budding. He had inherited his father's tenacity.

Chloe's coffee was scalding, yet Bob gulped it. He needed that drink, but there was nothing to be gained from delaying any further. After leaving Chloe a few cents, he approached Charles.

'Harry Charles?'

'Huh?' the runaway slurred.

'You're coming with me.'

Bob seized the crook's lapels, and forced him to his feet. Charles tried to push Bob away, but the manhunter grasped the criminal's wrist and twisted his arm around his back. It pleasured Bob to hear Charles cry out like a baby. Charles flailed his other arm pathetically, only for Bob to clasp that, too. He wrestled the other arm back and skilfully manacled the fugitive. Bob tightened the handcuffs as forcefully as he could. Their pinch made Charles squeal, adding to Bob's pleasure.

Bob could easily have shot Charles in the back, but Bob had come to enjoy the fight in making a quarry submit. He marched the runaway out by the scruff of his neck. Charles was a multiple murderer, and had not earned Bob's compassion.

Before exiting, he turned and winked at the landlady.

'Thanks, Candy.'

Chloe winked back. How did this dreamboat know her? she pondered. Chloe hoped he would be back soon.